You Can't Run
From Love

Kate Snowdon

Bella
BOOKS

2013

Printed in the United States of America on acid-free paper
First published 2013

Cover Designer: Linda Callaghan

ISBN 13: 978-1-59493-314-1

Dedication

For Gerry. Would you believe it?

Acknowledgment

Many thanks to Bella for accepting this book in the first place and to Karin for her welcoming cheerfulness and much-needed advice. Also to my editor for her patience, despite scaring me to death with the work I had to do to hopefully make this book an enjoyable read. My thanks also go out to Fiona for reading every word I wrote, a very brave woman. And to Linda, who did the dishes that night.

About the Author

A teacher once asked me, "What do you want to be when you grow up?" Unlike my friends, I didn't have a clue and thought I couldn't go far wrong if I followed in my parents' footsteps. "Actress," I replied. Then came the inevitable sigh from the teacher. "Kate, that is not a proper job." I liked the idea, but after my one and only performance, I knew it wasn't for me. I've come up with many ideas since then, some more successful than others. Waitress to assistant hotel manager, farmer to zoologist and out of desperation, thinking I really needed to settle on something, nurse, then on to my present position in clinical research. Fortunately though, despite my teacher, I didn't curtail my need to try different things, otherwise I wouldn't be on the writing adventure I'm now on. And I certainly wouldn't have made it from England, via Wales to Scotland, to the place that has provided me with so much outdoor and relaxing pleasure. In truth, I hope I will never know what I want to be when I grow up.

CHAPTER ONE

Reaching the bottom of the wooded hill Jess Brewster unhooked the gate and gave a contented sigh. She had walked that path for thirty-five years and had never tired of the changes each season brought. Stamping the snow off her boots, her pace became an easier stride as she headed through the gate and down the narrow lane toward the village. Covered in a thin patchwork of snow, slush and ice, it was a contrast to just a few days ago when it was all snow. Smiling, she admired the surrounding countryside that was her home. It wasn't difficult to understand the allure for winter walkers, climbers and skiers, looking at the pure white mountains surrounding her. Jess, although well qualified to navigate them as a trained mountain rescuer, preferred the lower hills and glens in winter, with their more diverse landscapes, trees and wildlife. She left the rugged open mountains to the warmer times of the year. Today the mountains would be very popular. The sky was blue with not a cloud in sight and Jess could feel a little warmth on her cheeks from the sun.

She looked up the lane and watched as the birds chased each other in and out of the bare hedgerow and green-tinged trees on either side of her. The freezing, wintry feel of just a few days ago was definitely breaking into spring, though only barely. The biting breeze that had been a constant this winter still remained, especially along the lane that acted like the perfect wind tunnel. Jess pulled her hat lower over her ears and her scarf up over her mouth.

Black Loch, a fair-sized body of water and the halfway point between the gate and Jock's Bridge, on the edge of the village, had been frozen for almost two months. She was pleased to see it not looking white in parts, an indication it was beginning to thaw. She hoped it wouldn't be too long before the bright yellow flowers of the primrose, could be seen clinging to its edges.

Looking back to the top of the wooded hill, she could just about make out one side of a lodge. It was the only time of year, before the larch grew their needles again, that you could see Woodland Lodges from any distance. It comprised of twelve lodges in total and they had been full throughout the season. Most years there would be a little respite in November and February, but the abundance of snow this year had kept the visitors coming. The lodges had a reputation for first-class accommodation and excellent access for many outdoor pursuits. Nobody went away from their holiday disappointed.

The current success of the business though, had been severely overshadowed by her uncle's illness. The diagnosis of stomach cancer, late last summer, had led to surgery, chemotherapy and then radiation. The radiation had been the worst part of the treatment and Uncle Jack had been glad to see the last of it. Her large, robust uncle, full of energy and enthusiasm for life, had suffered. He had loathed feeling so unwell and useless, but the last three weeks had seen him improve on a daily basis. Jess hoped his now thin and frail frame would strengthen. She strode happily toward the village. *Things are definitely looking up.*

***

Rachel Cummings was finding the last few miles of her journey to Woodland Lodges stressful. The main roads had been clear and easy to negotiate but she had left those behind at the ruins of Duilach Castle. Reaching that particular landmark usually pleased her and always made her smile. The road ran right up to what was obviously a tower, and then curved its way around the perimeter of the site. It was if they hadn't been looking up when they'd laid the tarmac. But the winding, narrow roads that followed, that indicated her journey was close to an end, were not welcome on this occasion. She was not used to driving in ice or snow and knew she was probably being overcautious. Usually, she would be giddy with anticipation at starting her annual, five-month retreat at Woodland Lodges. Today, she just wanted to get there in one piece. Normally she would be here from late May to October. This year though, her sister was getting married in August, so it made more sense to come a little earlier. She would then stay in New York, as there was a strong possibility she'd have to go to London later in the year. Rachel had developed a comfortable routine over the last six years, splitting her year between her home in the States and the lodges in Scotland. Another three or four weeks would be spent visiting her father and friends in the English capital.

As she passed through the last, very familiar village, her spirits began to lift, along with the tension in her neck and the stiffness in her fingers from gripping the steering wheel. She slowly took the Jeep around the sharp bend at Jock's Bridge, toward the long stretch of road before the eight-mile, wood-lined track, up to Woodland Lodges. In the distance she saw a figure walking toward her, who moved over to stand on the snow-covered edge. In return, Rachel slowed and maneuvered her Jeep over to the opposite side of the lane. As she passed they waved to each other and to Rachel's horror an arc of mud and slush flew up from the tires and covered the bystander from head to toe. She couldn't have made a better hit if she'd aimed.

Jess cursed as the Jeep continued by. She glared at the retreating monster, spitting out muck and hopelessly brushing at the crud that covered her face and body. Then to her astonishment the brake lights went on, followed by the white reversing lights. The driver's door then opened and a woman climbed out and gingerly walked toward her, excitedly apologizing. Jess just stood and stared, her sudden flash of anger gone as quickly as it had erupted. She was amazed that anyone other than a local would stop, and the woman most definitely was not from around these parts. She oozed class, style, sophistication and was definitely very appealing to the eye.

Rachel grew concerned. The woman had not moved or said a word. Maybe the Jeep had shot a stone at her, stunning her in some bizarre fashion or she was just waiting to throttle her. Rachel asked urgently, "Are you all right?"

Jess was grinning to herself. *That T-shirt in this weather really should have a hazard warning attached to it.* Her eyes had involuntarily moved over the driver's body, noting that all the curves were in all the right places, and then her gaze had settled on the stranger's nipples. The T-shirt clung to every contour. Her breasts were perfectly formed and an ample handful, but the reaction to the cold as she stepped out of the Jeep, produced those teasingly large nipples...*For goodness sake get a grip.* "Um sorry, yes, I'm fine thanks. I'm just amazed you stopped."

Rachel frowned. "I beg your pardon?" She couldn't believe anyone would think she would be so rude as to continue on her way.

"No, sorry, that's not what I meant." Jess was flustered. She blurted, to her dismay. "You'd better get yourself back to the Jeep, you're obviously cold."

Aware of where the woman's eyes had rested, Rachel crossed her arms. A deep red blush flooded the woman's mud-splattered face. All Rachel could do was smile. "With your trousers that wet you'll freeze. Can I give you a lift?"

"No, it's all right, thank you." Jess indicated with a nod. "There's a tractor heading our way and you're pointed in the wrong direction."

Rachel turned to look, a slightly panicked expression on her face. "Oh no."

"Go on, I'll be fine. The farmers around here are not known for their patience." Jess smirked, as Rachel quickly moved toward her Jeep, tiptoeing once again to avoid slipping or getting her feet wet.

***

Mark shouted above the engine's noise as he opened the cabin door. "Hi Jess, want a lift?"

"Thanks." Jess climbed aboard the tractor with a struggle, fighting trousers and long johns that were plastered to her thighs.

Mark's eyes widened and his mouth dropped open. "What happened to you? Don't tell me it was that Jeep, I could have edged them into the ditch for you."

Jess laughed and rolled her eyes. "Believe it or not she actually stopped to apologize."

"Well that must be a first." He looked her up and down with a grin. "Your face is covered in mud. Here, give it a wipe." Mark tossed her a damp cloth.

She inspected it closely. "This clean?"

He chuckled as he started toward the village. "It's only condensation from the windshield."

Jess wiped her face. "You heading back soon?"

"I'm collecting some materials from Farley's so I'll only be about an hour. Want a lift home?"

"That would be great, thanks. I don't fancy the walk back now. How does my face look?"

He made a point of looking intently and then screwed up his nose. "Ugly as ever."

Mark was forty-six, five years older than Jess, and although they had spent time in each other's company when they were young, they hadn't seen themselves as friends, until he was in his late twenties, when age didn't matter so much. Mark had gone into farming as soon as he'd turned sixteen and still worked the same farm. He was now a well-respected manager for his elderly employer.

The tractor pulled up outside the store and Jess jumped down. "Thanks, I'll see you later."

***

The store sat in the center of the village serving the local community with fresh produce, emergency dry goods, newspapers, a small selection of liquor, and the all-important post office. The connecting building was the doctor's surgery with its own dispensary. The rest of the village, which nestled close to the edge of the river and at the foot of one of the many glens in the area, consisted of around thirty houses scattered along one main road, a public house and a small cemetery. It was a picturesque place with its old stone buildings. Every space was filled with trees or shrubs and in the summer, gardens were a welcoming mass of blooming colors, enjoyed by both the locals and tourists alike.

Jess chuckled as the bell above the door tinkled to announce her presence. It wasn't long ago that Julie, the owner of the store and her best friend, since their ages were in single figures, had temporarily dispensed with the bell. Last summer a couple of visiting youths had stopped it from ringing as they entered and were caught only by chance, pilfering goods. Julie had then installed a buzzer that couldn't be tampered with. The noise of it every time they entered drove the locals mad and if Julie was honest, herself as well. After reasoning that it was only the one time she'd had any trouble and they hadn't got away with anything, she had reinstated the bell, much to everyone's delight. "Hi Julie, it's only me."

"Hi Jess," came a reply from behind one of the small well-stocked shelves. "How are you?" Julie rounded the end of the aisle with her arms open for a hug. Jess stepped forward only to have the arms in front of her drop suddenly and her friend step back. "Oh no, you don't. What on earth happened to you? You're soaked and filthy."

Jess shook her head. "Don't forget to add cold. And no, I didn't fall before you ask."

"Come on. Get those clothes off, before you freeze." Julie beckoned to Jess impatiently.

Jess followed. "Now there's an offer I can't refuse. Did you have something in mind to warm me up? I'd be more than happy to provide you with a few pointers."

Julie turned around, walked seductively toward her friend and uttered in a low and sultry voice, "Who said I would need any pointers. I'm sure I could teach you a thing or two." Her eyebrows rose up and down, before they both burst into laughter.

Julie grabbed an arm. "Come on, I'll find you something dry to change into. Just put every wet thing by the fire and they might dry a little before you have to go."

Jess did as instructed. She loved this little room behind the shop counter—nothing matched. It contained a sofa and armchair that were draped in tartan blankets and huddled close to a small open fire. On the floor were numerous rugs, covering a loud green carpet of swirling patterns. The rest of the room provided functional furniture and equipment for use when the shop was open.

"Here we are," Julie cried, flapping a pair of joggers about her head.

Jess looked suspiciously at her. "Whose are those?" Julie was a good three inches smaller than she, and Tom, her husband, was about four inches taller and much broader.

"They're yours, believe it or not. I'd forgotten I had them."

Jess frowned. "I don't remember those. Oh, wait a minute, I lent you those when…" She smirked.

"Yes, it was the day I was attempting to help you unblock that sewage drain." Julie threw them at Jess. "Change woman, before your legs freeze." Jess laughed and peeled off her long johns.

Tom walked in, placing a package on a nearby desk. "Well this is a greeting, any more coming off?"

His wife punched him playfully in the arm. "Behave."

Jess had a glint in her eye. "I'm not usually caught with my pants down by someone's other half."

"Jess Brewster!" Julie raised an eyebrow and folded her arms across her chest.

She quickly pulled on the joggers while Tom wrapped his arms around Julie's waist, chuckling. "Those legs look far too cold to get close to. You're a much warmer bet."

Tom was the senior partner in a practice of two doctors that cared for the local community and its visitors. He kissed Julie tenderly then turned to Jess, nodding toward her legs. "What have you been up to anyway? Legs really shouldn't be that color."

She moved to stand in front of the fire. "A passing motorist." He waited for more.

Jess grinned. "I'm only telling it once and someone will want a lot more detail than you."

They both looked at Julie. "You're right. Best of luck, I'll hear it later."

Julie glared, first at her husband and then at Jess. "I won't ask now."

Tom winked at Jess and then patted the package he had brought in with him. "Marcus saw you arrive. This is Jack's medicine. Sorry I didn't have it organized for you on Saturday."

"Please don't worry, he hasn't run out. You know how cautious I am."

"I know, but you have more than enough to do without having to make another trip here so soon."

Jess wandered over to him and linked her arm through his. "It's fine, I enjoyed the walk, despite my wee bit of bother, and I have a list for Julie anyway." She smiled. "Thanks for bringing it through. I'm just going to go and wash up."

When she returned a few minutes later, Tom had gone back through to the practice next door, and Julie was busy in the shop filling her backpack.

Julie looked up. "I take it that list in your trouser pocket, were the items you needed?"

"Yes, thanks. I'll go make us a cup of tea if you have that under control."

Just as the tea was poured, Julie entered the little room and looked at her friend of thirty years and more. The usual, unruly mop of red, curly hair had been flattened by her hat. She couldn't resist putting her fingers through it, in an attempt to make it bounce back up. "I'll never understand why you insist on hiking down here, when you have a perfectly good truck and Range Rover."

Jess chuckled. "I only do it when I'm picking up relatively few items. I just don't see the point in traveling almost ten miles when you can do it in just over two?" That was the distance from the gate on the lane to Woodland Lodges via the footpath. The road took a long loop up. Jess could easily beat a car coming down, but going back up the hillside was a little hit-and-miss.

"Okay." Julie started tugging at a wet trouser leg hanging just beside her. "So what exactly happened?"

Jess gave her the full story and as usual nothing could be left out. Julie couldn't help but laugh. "I can't believe you commented on her nipples. You were lucky she didn't slap you."

Jess blushed. "I didn't mention her nipples."

"Well you might just as well have, it's not good getting caught taking a peek." Julie chuckled, raising her eyebrows. "After a gaffe like that, you should have just gone all the way and asked her where she was staying, especially if she was that attractive. Do you think you might have missed your chance, do you think she was a lesbian?"

Jess rolled her eyes. "How on earth would I know that?"

"Your gaydar." Julie laughed.

Jess stuck her tongue out. "What gaydar? Mine only works if I'm in a gay bar and a woman starts talking sex with me."

"You found her attractive, doesn't that count for something?"

Jess shook her head. "Yes, but *durr*, some good-looking women are straight you know."

"Very funny. You really are hopeless. You could have been that woman's holiday romance." She winked at Jess and they both laughed.

An image suddenly sprang into Jess's mind of sliding a hand through that gorgeous mane of thick brown hair, while her other hand gently took a breast and teased one of those very inviting nipples. She sighed, feeling a sudden throb of heat between her thighs. She looked at Julie. "Now that I could handle, and I'm sure it would be most enjoyable."

Julie nodded. "She was that attractive then?"

Jess instantly felt uncomfortable. She usually wasn't so obvious in her desire of another. "Anything would appear attractive to me at the moment, it's been a while. After today's reaction, I think I should get out more."

CHAPTER TWO

Rachel heaved a contented sigh as she sank into the large comfortable sofa and gazed out the glass doors of the lounge and beyond the balcony. The view never bored her, even after six years. Trees and shrubs had matured but the birds flittering around the feeders and the squirrels jumping from branch to branch were unchanged. The difference this year, though, was that she could see more. Usually, it would only be the five peaks along the undulating ridge that were visible behind the trees. Their dark craggy edges and deep ravines, making them look forbidding. The snow changed that completely. They looked soft and rounded, very much like the rolling, lower-lying hills in summer that, Rachel mused, looked like giant green sponges.

Usually she would only see glimpses of the hills from here, through branches full of leaves and needles. But this time she could see whole mountain and hill faces, making it easier to imagine the varying shades of purple that showed when the heather bloomed in late summer. Something she would miss this year.

Rachel looked upon the lodge as her second home. It was a place far removed from city life, a perfect balance to that busy, demanding lifestyle.

After arriving midafternoon she had been greeted by Marie, who was the live-in housekeeper and overseer for the cleaning of the lodges, and a very good friend to the inhabitants of the house. She had gained the position not long after Jack had become the sole guardian to Jess Brewster, after an accident had claimed their family. Marie had also been widowed and there were not many positions that welcomed a woman who had a young daughter. It had worked out well for them both. Rachel was amused to hear she was now engaged to Bill, the landlord of the village pub. The pair had been courting for as long as Rachel had been coming here and she felt this development was way overdue.

The shock on her arrival had been Jack. He was a shadow of his former self, so much thinner and shrunken in stature. He had been a biggish man before his illness, with a strong presence. She smiled. He still had that twinkle of mischief in his eye and that wonderful enthusiasm for life that she always found uplifting. It was miraculous, considering what he'd obviously been through.

She had been invited to dinner as usual on her day of arrival. It had turned into a ritual they had grown accustomed to and enjoyed. This time would be different though; it would be her first meeting with Jack's niece and she was a little apprehensive. Usually Jess spent her summers as a walking guide for a holiday company, so their paths had never crossed. Jack loved his niece and was looking forward to the two of them finally meeting.

Don, an old friend of Jack's, and the hired help in the summer, had assisted with unloading her bags. She had unpacked most of her belongings then showered, and was now just waiting to wander down to the house for dinner. Lomond Lodge was the farthest up the hillside of the lodges that were privately scattered around the forested estate of indigenous trees and pines. *I'll just wait another ten minutes.*

***

The meal was under control and Jess was deciding what to wear. She couldn't understand why she was nervous about meeting Rachel Cummings. Was it because she was a well-known children's illustrator and artist, or the fact she was American? Every American she had met had been confident and a little overpowering. Jess tutted at her prejudice. She hadn't met that many. It wasn't that. It was the fact that Uncle Jack had always spoken so highly of her and was obviously very fond of her. She didn't want to disappoint him by not liking this woman.

***

"Evening Rachel, come in, let me take your coat." Jack stepped aside to let her pass.

She smiled. "Thank you."

"Go on through to the lounge. Don, Jean and Marie are already in there."

Jean was Don's wife, whom Rachel knew well. The women fell easily into conversation, while Don tended to the drinks.

Jack popped his head around the kitchen door. Jess was busy with her preparations for dinner. When it was more than the three of them Jess tended to make the meals. Marie found dinners a chore and Jess loved the chance to cook. "Rachel's arrived. Could you spare a few minutes to say hello?"

She turned around, happy to see her uncle buzzing about. "Yes, that's fine, everything's ready here."

She followed her uncle into the lounge as he interrupted the group huddled around the fireplace. "Sorry to disturb you all. I'd just like to make some introductions. Rachel, this is Jess. Jess, this is Rachel."

Jess froze, her mouth agape. *Of all the people.* Then to her dismay, Rachel uncontrollably uttered, "Great."

Quickly regaining her composure Jess walked toward the diminutive, dark-haired woman. Smiling ruefully, she extended her hand in greeting. "I'm really very sorry, Rachel, that was more than rude. Believe me, it is a pleasure to finally meet you." She winked. "Properly."

Rachel relaxed, returning the smile and took Jess's hand. "Are you sure?"

There were a number of puzzled looks exchanged around the room. Rachel looked at them. "Did Jess tell you what happened to her this afternoon?"

There was a momentary silence before Marie chuckled and piped up. "She didn't have to say anything. It was all over her."

The room broke into laughter and Rachel looked back at Jess. "I am sorry."

"Forget it. It'll keep them entertained for weeks." She gave a mischievous grin. "Mind you, if you hadn't stopped, I certainly wouldn't be telling you to forget it."

***

The meal was a delicious affair and the chat among the group had been easy. Jess brought in the coffee and sat back quietly in her chair.

While the others continued their discussion, Rachel took the chance to appraise the first woman in years to have piqued her interest. She had not said a great deal throughout the meal but had responded brightly when required. Rachel couldn't detect a moody personality, only one that appeared relaxed, thoughtful and content with herself. Jess was certainly more attractive than any of the pictures Jack had shown her. Her red hair was a mass of curls, which contrasted beautifully with the blue eyes that cheekily sparkled whenever a grin or smile adorned her face. Her height, four to five inches taller than Rachel's five feet four, was emphasized by a lean muscular build.

"Rachel, the exhibition you have on this summer in Glasgow, who are the other artists showing with you?" Don asked.

She quickly focused her attention. "Oh Don, there are a number of them. I hate to admit it, but I only actually know a couple of them."

The conversation then naturally continued on the art theme, as it had so many times when Don and Jean were present. The two of them had taken up painting on Jean's retirement and had become so-called experts on the subject. Jess smiled to herself. Here was a real artist and they were trying to compete with her knowledge. *I wonder if this happens every year.* She looked over at Rachel, who was joking and laughing. Jess had found it difficult not to look at her for most of the evening and was trying to fathom out why. She chuckled. It could have something to do with her being gorgeous. There was a sudden lull in the conversation and everyone looked her way, including Rachel, with a grin on her face. She quickly sat up. *Oh God, did she say something to me?*

Don laughed. "I wouldn't ask Jess, she has no idea."

Jess frowned, looking back at everyone. "Don't ask me what?"

"Are there any particular artists that you like?" Rachel said.

Jess shuffled in her chair. "Um, not really, it depends more on the painting and if I like the look of it."

"Jess wouldn't know a good artist from a bad one," Don goaded.

Jack interjected. "That isn't true. Jess has some wonderful pictures hanging about this house and you know it."

"Well she won't pay more than fifty pounds for a painting and you don't get good artists for that price."

Jess knew things would become heated. They always did when they discussed this topic. Uncle Jack appeared to get some gleeful pleasure out of winding him up. *Well I can't blame him. A rugged Scotsman and art really don't marry.* But on this occasion she felt the need to defuse it.

"Don's right, I'm a heathen when it comes to art." She smiled at him. "We have this argument quite frequently. I don't like to pay a fortune for a picture, despite knowing the effort and materials involved."

Marie added. "Fifty pounds? You consider that a fortune? You're getting cheap, Jess. Or turning into a true Scot—watching your pennies."

There were a few chuckles and Rachel thought that what could have been a difficult moment had passed without real incident. These people were used to each other. But she was surprised at her irritation with Don. It had never occurred to her before that he was such a snob.

Art wasn't mentioned again, except when everyone was trying to remember the name of Christie Brinkley's first husband, who happened to be a well-known French artist. Jess had sat quietly again and then casually dropped Jean-François Allaux into the conversation. *Touché*, Rachel thought.

As they settled in the lounge, attention once again was focused on Rachel. "What about the new Michelle Whitely book? You haven't mentioned that," Jean said excitedly.

Rachel smiled with effort. "Oh, that's not going to be until the end of the year. Actually, dates will be set in the next couple of weeks."

"You must be thrilled, though? What a comeback. Did you ever think there would be another one after so long?"

Rachel looked at the expectant faces. She had been the illustrator in the Kate Heavenly books, a series of popular children's adventures. The last one had been almost seven years ago and Michelle Whitely, the author, had resurrected the character in the hope of boosting her dwindling popularity. Persuaded by her agent, Rachel had accepted the invitation to be illustrator again. A move her agent thought would be good for her career. She was not convinced. "No, I thought she'd finished with the character altogether, years ago."

Jean rubbed her hands together. "I can't wait; I took the old ones to Australia for the grandchildren and they loved them."

Don rolled his eyes. "You mean *you* loved them, you always did."

They all chuckled as Jess watched Rachel. *She isn't enjoying this.*

***

The end of the evening arrived and when Don and Jean moved to leave, so did Rachel. They offered her a lift up the hill, but she refused as it was silly when she could walk. Jack then suggested Jess escort her.

"It's going to freeze again tonight," Jess said as she walked beside Rachel holding the torch out in front.

Rachel grinned. She was feeling a little lightheaded from the wine and long drive. "Why are the British so obsessed with discussing the weather whenever there's a lull in the conversation?"

Jess laughed. "I have absolutely no idea. But to change the subject, I can't believe I didn't work out who you were on the road this afternoon. I assumed you would have had an American accent, so I never even thought. It's funny how you conjure up pictures of people from other's descriptions."

"Oh don't, I'm worse. I've seen numerous pictures of you and didn't recognize you at all."

"That could've had something to do with my muddy disguise."

"That's not fair, and I don't think so. It was that woolen hat, hiding your hair."

Jess raised an eyebrow and looked at Rachel. "Is that my only distinguishing feature?"

Rachel deliberately turned to examine Jess. "You're right. It's only one of them."

Jess instantly blushed.

Rachel smiled and then continued to walk. She wasn't sure if she'd witnessed another blush. It was too dark to be sure.

"You do know Mark, don't you? Don and Jean's eldest son."

"Yes. Why?"

"Mark was in the tractor. I'm surprised he didn't recognize you."

"I don't usually have a Jeep with tinted glass. That could have something to do with it."

"Ah yes, a Suzuki," Jess said idly.

"Are you trying to say I'm predictable now?" Rachel teased.

"No. I'm not. I just happen to know that's what you like.

When you're here at least. I'm very predictable with my choice of vehicle. It's a Range Rover every time."

They walked in silence until Jess had the urge to fill it again. Although, not with the weather this time. "You didn't seem too happy about illustrating the new Kate Heavenly adventure."

"Was it that obvious?"

Jess suddenly felt a little awkward. "Well, I…I'm sorry I didn't mean to pry."

"You didn't pry, you made an observation. I'll have to be more careful." Realizing what she had said she added, "This is coming out all wrong. Would you mind if we dropped it?"

Curious as to why the topic of the book would be off limits, Jess mischievously pressed on against her better judgment. "I must admit I was never a great fan. The illustrations I did enjoy, though."

"Maybe it had something to do with your age?"

Jess noticed the clipped response. "Very funny. I was reading them under strict orders from Emma, Mark's daughter. She loved the series and kept reading them well into her teens I might add."

Rachel relaxed a little, this was safer territory. "So what didn't you like about them?"

"Oh. Kate."

"The hero?"

Jess nodded. "Too self-obsessed. She was always right, and far too nicey-nicey for my liking. I'm sure she would've got away with murder, if she was so inclined."

Rachel laughed. "She was a child and an orphan. So it's inevitable she's going to be perfect."

Jess grunted. "She used people and was manipulative. It was subtle, but she did."

Rachel's heart suddenly began racing in panic. She was describing Michelle Whitely. "Please, let's just drop this."

Puzzled, Jess scolded herself for taking her curiosity too far. *Why?* They were only discussing a character. Weren't they?

CHAPTER THREE

It was the first day of May and snow could be seen only on the very high mountains. Rachel was pleased. Spring had definitely arrived.

She was heading back to the lodge, having spent an hour or so with Jack, who had grown tired on this particular visit. Since her arrival she had taken afternoon tea on a number of occasions with him. This year she was determined to make them more frequent while he recovered.

She couldn't help feeling sadness for a man she had grown so fond of. He struggled heroically with his deteriorating health and his present frustration at not being able to help his niece.

The winter had been a never-ending fight for the three of them at Woodland Lodges. Don and Jean always spent the winter months visiting their two younger children and grandchildren in Australia and were presently making final arrangements for their emigration later in the year. Jack had been so pleased when they had returned, only for Don to slip a disc in his back the day after their dinner together. He did say he felt Don had been slowing down this last couple of years, but not being available at all would make it difficult, especially for Jess.

I'd be a little slow at seventy-two, Rachel thought. She did understand Jack's concern though. He and Jess usually managed to do all the major repairs and maintenance over the quieter winter months, so that the place would tick over more easily in the summer when visitors were plentiful and Jess went off to pursue other interests. He and Don always managed fine, but with Jack's illness and the lodges as busy as they had been this winter, the usual upkeep had not been done. Now Jess was having to prioritize jobs on a daily basis and was never really catching up. Still, she never appeared to be discontent.

As Rachel was passing the end of the drive to Earn Lodge she heard an almighty crash. She knew the family that had been staying there had left this morning and no one else was due until tomorrow. She hurried up the drive to find Jess in a tractor, with a gate suspended in the air.

Jess popped her head outside the cabin and yelled. "Don't come any closer just for a minute, please."

Rachel waved her compliance and once the offending gate was moved to the side, Jess jumped down from the tractor, a grin adorning her face.

"Hi, how you doing?"

Rachel couldn't help it and grinned back. "Fine, I came to see what the noise was."

Jess turned and indicated the gate posts. "I'm trying to change the gate. I stupidly completed it in the barn, thinking Don would be here to help me hang it. If I'd known he'd be lying on his back, I'd have done it on-site."

Rachel frowned. "Aren't they always made up beforehand anyway?"

"Only if you buy them that way." She then thought of the advantages. "Mind you if I'd done that, then two lovely, great hulking brutes would've come with it and hanged it for me."

Rachel laughed. "You're maybe too handy for your own good then. Could I help at all?"

She received a smirk. "I don't think so."

Rachel was affronted. "How do you know? I might be just as capable as you." Realizing the ridiculousness of the statement she relaxed and added, "Well, maybe not."

"It's not that I don't think you're capable. Marie would skin me alive if I had a visitor helping me out."

Rachel grunted. "I'm not any old visitor."

"You are in the eyes of Health and Safety."

"I won't sue, if you think I can help."

There was a pause. "Okay." Jess had an idea. If Rachel could slowly lower the winch on the tractor, they could probably place the gate onto its hinges.

She gave Rachel instructions and maneuvered the tractor near to the post, with the gate hanging close to where she wanted it. With Rachel using the winch and Jess tugging and pushing at the gate, they managed to get it just above the hinges. Suddenly Rachel screamed and the gate swung, knocking Jess off balance and almost trapping her leg as it hit the post.

Jess yelled, "Pull back on the lever, pull it back!"

When the gate stopped swinging she gave it a sweeping inspection and then rushed to the cab. *What are you doing checking the gate first, nothing like making a woman feel she's more important than a lump of wood.*

She jumped onto the sideboard to find Rachel shaking and with a vise-like grip on the lever. She reached into the cab and gently touched her arm. "It's okay, just engage the brake."

Rachel did as she was told and turned to Jess. "Oh God, I'm so sorry, are you okay?"

Jess smiled at the ghostly white face. "I'm fine, how about you?"

"Have I damaged anything?"

Jess winced and shook her head. "No. How about we try

again when the color returns to your face and those hands stop shaking?"

"You've got to be kidding!"

Jess chuckled and moved her hand from Rachel's arm to her hand and squeezed. "No. You did a fine job. It was only that last movement."

Rachel looked at her. Why on earth would she give her a second chance? She'd almost ruined her hard work and crushed her in the process. Jess suddenly jumped down from the tractor and winked. "We can do it."

***

Half an hour later, Jess handed Rachel a mug of tea and sat down beside her. She nodded toward the gate. "Looks good don't you think?"

"Does it open and close okay?"

"Perfectly, we did a grand job. Thanks." She tapped her mug against Rachel's before taking a sip.

They sat quietly looking at their handiwork, which in the end didn't take them long at all to complete. Rachel looked over at Jess. "I've been wanting to ask you something."

Jess gave her an inquisitive look. "What?"

"That first night, when you kindly walked me home, you said you had conjured up a picture of me from other people's descriptions." She raised an eyebrow. "What were you expecting?"

"Umm, I'm not sure. I don't know." Sighing, she continued. "I'll be honest. I usually work for this women's walking company in the summer, as a guide. There's often, quite a few well-off, middle-aged American women on them." She chuckled. "They tend to be a little more, err...forthright than most and don't necessarily beat around the bush when they have something to say. Much like some of the guests we get here." She cringed and quickly glanced at Rachel. "Not all of them I hasten to add."

"You thought I might be like that then?"

Jess fidgeted. How on earth had she got into this? "No not exactly, no one around here has a bad thing to say about you. As far as they're concerned, you're wonderful."

Rachel gave her a sideways glance. "And this made you skeptical?"

Jess mock pouted. "You're making fun of me?"

Rachel laughed. "No I'm not. You just obviously have a very biased view of Americans."

"Now you're being sarcastic. My experience is just limited, and I've been proved to be wrong on many occasions. Anyway, if Julie can still like you, after Tom let slip one drunken night what a lovely and attractive person he thinks you are and still be married to her, believe me, that is something. It conjures up a person who is almost perfect in every way."

Rachel looked a little embarrassed. "You've never heard a bad word about me in six years?"

Jess shook her head. "No." She grinned wickedly. "Except…"

Rachel nudged her with her shoulder. "Funny." And then had the urge to ask Jess if she found her as attractive as Tom had. Instead she said, "Just so that you have the full picture, I was born in America. I came to England with my parents when I was six, and shortly afterward my sister was born. My parents split up when I was fourteen, and I chose to stay with my father until I finished school. My mother and sister went back to the States. Since then, I've split my time between here and New York. At least, that is, once my mother got over my betrayal. My mother's American and my father's English."

Jess nodded, interested that Rachel was giving her this information. "And your career?"

Rachel smiled. "I went to the Royal College of Art and then became a reasonably successful illustrator, much too both my parents' disappointment…No, that's not the right word. Disillusionment, maybe. It's not what either of them had in mind for me."

"Are they happy with your choice now?"

"Fairly. My father's second wife is the most enthusiastic. My father wanted me to follow him into corporate business and my mother wanted me to be either a doctor, or married to a successful man. They both would have been happy if I'd been an accountant though."

Jess chuckled. "Umm. I can imagine, but maybe not as happy?"

"No, you're right. I like what I do."

Rachel wanted to ask Jess's history, but wasn't sure if the redhead would want to discuss how she came to live with her uncle. She knew the basic story. What she didn't know was anything about Jess as a person, only that she was loved and liked by those around her. She was too afraid to ask and Jess didn't volunteer the information.

***

Jack stepped into the conservatory. "You all right, Jess?"

"Yes. Why?" She turned around and smiled as her uncle handed her a mug of tea before easing himself down into one of the wicker chairs next to hers.

"You've sat here for the last twenty minutes, staring out of that window at nothing." He looked at his watch. "You're never here midmorning."

Jess often looked out of the window, usually the large one in their beloved observation room where she could watch the birds at the feeders. This one simply looked over to the yard. "I'm just a little tired and waiting for Mark. He should be along shortly. He's dropping off the wood I ordered from Farley's." She was lying. Well not entirely; she was tired and she was waiting for Mark, but her thoughts were somewhere else.

Jack stood. "Want some fruitcake?"

"That would be good, thanks. Want me to get it?"

He squeezed her shoulder. "No, you just sit there. I'll be back in a minute."

Jess sighed. Rachel had been here, what? Three and a half weeks? Apart from the dinner on her arrival and yesterday when she had helped her with the gate, they had spent very little time in each other's company. There was the occasional "Hi" and a quick chat, but that was all. Jess hadn't even intruded on her afternoon teas with her uncle. So why then was she thinking about her? Why was she getting a stupid giddy sensation every time she saw her? Why when she touched her in the cab had she felt a rush of heat? She closed her eyes. And why on earth had she invited her to dinner tonight? She groaned. It was supposed to be Jack's thank you to Tom and Julie for their support over the last few months.

"Why the groan?"

She jumped slightly before taking the offered cake. "Was it that loud?"

"Obviously because my hearing certainly isn't what it used to be."

Jess chuckled. "I've done a silly thing."

Jack tentatively asked, "What?"

She looked over at her uncle and took a deep breath. "I'm afraid I invited Rachel to dinner tonight."

Jack raised an eyebrow. "And the problem is?"

"It was supposed to be for Julie and Tom. A thank you."

"Yes, but I don't want to make a big deal of it, that would just embarrass them." He shrugged. "They know and like Rachel."

"I know, but that's not the point."

"I really can't see the problem." He paused. "Why did you invite her anyway?"

Jess relaxed a little and leaned over toward him and said conspiratorially, "Don't tell Marie, but she helped me with the gate at Earn Lodge."

"Oh." He looked disappointed and then said slightly irritated. "I thought Mark was going to help you with that?"

Jess dismissed her uncle's look. "He couldn't until this morning, and I didn't want to chance leaving it, so I was trying to do it myself."

"Good grief, Jess. Are you trying to kill yourself?"

"Rachel did a good job," she replied defensively.

He rolled his eyes. "Well you're both still in one piece I suppose. So I take it dinner is a thank you?"

"Right."

"Well, you said it yourself that it was a thank-you meal." Jack took her hand and smiled. "You worry too much."

CHAPTER FOUR

Rachel looked up at the roof. Jess hadn't noticed her. She was humming away to herself replacing a section of tiles that had been dislodged by a fallen tree. Rachel couldn't help but admire the gusto of this woman, who didn't appear to be afraid of anything. It was a cool, sunny day and Jess worked away in a pair of shorts and a T-shirt. She was beautifully slender with small breasts that pushed pertly against the fabric. A faint tan, which would only grow as the summer took hold, emphasized every muscle in endless arms and legs. Rachel imagined her whole body was just as firm. She shook her head, surprised she was imagining what it would be like to run her hands over that body. *In your dreams Rachel, you*

wouldn't know what to do with her. You'd probably bruise yourself
if you got that close.

Jess suddenly felt a presence and looked over her shoulder.
"Hi. Are you spying on me, or just waiting for me to fall?"

Rachel laughed. "I didn't want to shout out in case I startled
you. Jack would never forgive me if I was the cause of you
seriously injuring yourself."

Jess headed down the ladder. "I was just about to have a break.
Care to join me? I have a spare mug."

"Do you always carry two mugs?"

"Of course. You never know who might turn up and it's
always a good excuse for a break." Jess poured out two teas and
handed Rachel a large piece of carrot cake as she settled down on
a step leading up to Ness Lodge.

"Oh this is good, your handiwork or Marie's?"

"Cake, bread and puddings are Marie's department. I couldn't
keep up with the amount we consume. I may have the biggest
appetite, but Marie and Uncle Jack eat their fair share." Jess
frowned. "Maybe not so much Uncle Jack, but his appetite has
definitely improved lately." She gazed at the open space of where
the tree had fallen. "How do you think he looks?"

Unsure of what she should say, Rachel decided such an open
question deserved an honest answer. "I was shocked at first. He's
lost an incredible amount of weight. But it's good to see the
sparkle in his eyes is still there."

Jess continued to look at nothing in particular. "Yes."

Rachel felt the need to say something, but didn't really know
what, so she offered to help. It succeeded in diverting Jess's
thoughts as they decided Rachel could start loading the wood
onto the trailer, along with the materials no longer required. Jess
said, "It's not that I don't trust you up on the roof—"

"But if Marie caught me up there, she'd skin you alive."

"Something like that." Jess smiled at Rachel. "You know,
you're exposing a lot of prejudices, I never realized I had."

Pulling on a pair of work gloves Rachel asked, "Besides me
being American, what do you mean?"

Jess chuckled. "You're not going to let that drop are you?"

"I might, it depends what you're going to say now."

"The way you tiptoed through the snow that first day, in your walking boots, I..."

Rachel glared playfully. "You thought I was all show and incapable of anything truly physical?"

Jess coughed and turned to hide her reddening face. "You'll just have to prove me wrong."

***

Later, as Rachel was loading the last of the logs onto the trailer, Jess could only admire her. It was obvious she wasn't used to physical labor, although she was reasonably fit and certainly in good shape. Very good shape. Her enthusiasm was great and far outweighed the lack of experience. Also for someone who always looked impeccable, she wasn't afraid to get dirty either. Jess shook her head in astonishment. Even dirty she looked neat and tidy. How on earth could one person be so perfect? She looked Rachel up and down and wiggled her eyebrows. Yes, perfect. All rounded in exactly the right places.

Rachel suddenly stopped and looked her way. Flustered at being caught, Jess croaked, "Not much more to load, I'll come and give you a hand."

An awkward silence engulfed them and Jess was convinced Rachel could read her mind. *Say something.* "I believe you're going to Edinburgh on Sunday?"

Rachel paused, stretching her back as she looked at Jess. "Yes, there's a meeting with the publishers first thing Monday morning, regarding the release of the book. Then I'm meeting a couple of friends who've never been before. I'm looking forward to showing them the sites. Apparently, our first stop is to be the castle, they want to see if it's as amazing as it's portrayed. Sitting high on that rock and overlooking the city below. London's full of history, but it's palpable in Edinburgh and they love that sort of thing and so do I."

Jess nodded at Rachel's excitement. "It is a beautiful city and that sounds like a good plan, getting business out of the way first so that you can enjoy it."

"Yes, especially when you're not particularly looking forward to it." She glanced quickly at Jess, hoping she wouldn't pry any further into the book publishing situation. Thankfully, this time she seemed preoccupied with other thoughts.

CHAPTER FIVE

"Jess, that's Rose and Mark pulling up."

Jess grabbed her bag and went through to the conservatory. "Told you they'd be here. I'll see you tomorrow."

Jack pecked her on the cheek. "Enjoy yourself."

She smiled at his frown. "I will." He'd been annoyed at her for not mentioning the party. It's not that she'd deliberately omitted to mention it, she just wasn't entirely sure about spending a night away from home at the moment. Julie hadn't realized this when she'd asked her uncle if Jess was looking forward the céilidh.

***

Mark sounded a little anxious when she jumped into the back of the Land Rover. "Now Jess, we're going to drop you and Julie off at the party first and then take your bags to the hotel. It's just the other way around from what we planned."

"Don't worry. It's good of you to give us a lift."

Mark and his wife Rose laughed in unison before Rose said, "Too late, we're already worried. We just want to be prepared with our strategy before we pick Julie up. And we'll need you on our side."

"Don't tell me you're frightened of her?"

Again, they replied in unison. "Yes."

They all chuckled and Jess, agreed that it probably was the best plan to pacify Julie, who would be panicking at this very moment.

A little over an hour later they entered the outskirts of town. Julie looked at her watch. "Are we nearly there, Rose?"

Jess patted her knee. "We have plenty of time, stop pestering the driver."

Julie glared before looking anxiously ahead. "I don't want to be late. They said to be there by eight thirty, it's supposed to be a surprise, remember." She looked back at her friend. "I thought we'd decided on your black shirt for tonight?"

Jess raised an eyebrow. "*You* decided on my black shirt. It's a céilidh, a family one. I don't want to look like I'm on the..." She stopped. "I don't want to stick out."

Mark turned around with a mischievous look on his face. "You still look very good Jess, and you're right, you wouldn't want to give Maddie the wrong idea."

Rose elbowed him in the side. "Mark."

Jess looked from Julie to the two grinning faces in the front, as Julie quickly looked out the side window. She frowned and tugged at Julie's arm. "What's this about Maddie? Is she here?"

Julie turned around. "It's her brother's birthday party. Of course she's going to be there. Why wouldn't she be?"

"She lives in Canada."

"She came back a few weeks ago and plans on staying. She's finally left her husband." Julie quickly added. "Didn't you know?"

Blue eyes narrowed as Jess said, "I would have, if you'd mentioned it. Now, please don't tell me you were trying to match-make?"

Julie swallowed nervously. "Well, you used to like her."

"I had a schoolgirl crush and her reputation leaves a lot to be desired. Are you sure it wasn't her husband that left her?"

Julie crossed her arms defensively. "Apparently she's changed and now knows what she wants out of life."

"Who told you that? Her mother?"

Julie turned toward the window again. Jess gripped her knee. "Oh Julie, that's a bit desperate if you're looking at Maddie as a girlfriend for me."

They all laughed except for Julie, who asked, "Have you heard of any encounters she's had recently?" She looked around at all three them. Jess couldn't answer. Rose and Mark shook their heads. "See, a changed woman."

Jess shook her head. "All right, a changed woman since she's discovered she prefers women to men. It's good of you Julie, but I think I'll give her a miss or at least, a lot more time."

Julie conceded. "Well maybe that was a little desperate, I just want…"

Jess smiled reassuringly. "I'm perfectly happy. I wish you'd quit worrying yourself. You're getting worse."

"No. I just care."

***

The bar was heaving and the dancing was in full flow. Strip the Willow was one dance Jess always loved to watch. It was rare that someone didn't get tangled up and confused in those turns. As usual there were more men in skirts than there were women. The two Macleod tartans were the most common on show tonight, but there was still a good variation of tartans swaying about. It always amused Jess that when the men wore their kilts they tended to strut like proud peacocks. She clapped with a little difficulty as the dance ended and spotted Julie approaching. She linked her arm through Jess's and looked up at her. "Hi you."

Jess politely excused herself from the woman who was fawning over her and turned to Julie, mouthing "Thanks," as she was guided toward a couple of empty chairs.

"Are you enjoying yourself?" Julie asked as they both sat down.

"Not too bad. How about you?"

"I'm getting too old, or I'm too married, for this sort of thing. Everyone appears to be divorced or unhappy and on the prowl for a potential fling."

They both laughed. "That could be a slight exaggeration Jules, but I have to say I know what you mean. Predators would be a good word." They laughed again.

"Do you think we've all reached the age for a midlife crisis? Maybe I should see if I've still got it."

Again they laughed and Jess said, "We're finding an awful lot funny this evening."

Julie leaned forward conspiratorially. "I think that could have something to do with the alcohol."

Shuffling her seat toward Julie, Jess asked, "You reckon?" Then frowned. "This chair's a bit wobbly."

This time their laughter was uncontrollable until two large glasses of red wine appeared. The waitress indicated to a woman a few tables away, who dipped her head, looking directly at Jess and produced an incredibly seductive smile. Jess nodded their thanks without returning a smile of any kind.

Julie leaned on Jess's knees for support. "Is that nodding some sort of code and why didn't you smile back?"

Jess grinned at her friend. "Don't start me off again. It's just a power thing."

She looked at Jess quizzically. "I didn't think you were into that sort of thing?"

"Not me, those two." She looked toward the woman at the bar and then the source of the drinks. "I haven't had to buy a drink all night."

Julie suddenly looked pleased with herself. "Yes, you have, you bought me one. Do I win?"

Jess smiled and teasingly said, "Well yes, if you want to join me in my bed tonight?"

Julie slowly closed and opened her eyes, desperately trying to mimic a disapproving look, but failed miserably. "So those two bees are fighting over the honey pot are they?" She started chuckling. "Either take your fancy?"

"Nah. Unfortunately."

"Why unfortunately?"

"Forget it."

"No. Are you feeling horny and neither one is suitable?"

"Julie!" Jess screeched as she looked around for eavesdroppers.

"Well you haven't been out since you returned last summer, so it wouldn't be surprising."

"Good grief woman, are you keeping tabs on me? I'll have you know, I don't get that desperate."

Julie winked. "Nothing escapes me my friend."

They both giggled and then sat quietly. "Could I ask you something without you jumping to a conclusion?"

Julie's interest piqued. "Of course you can. You know you can."

"Umm." Jess looked a little skeptical at the bleary gaze she was receiving. "Do you think Rachel is…you know, like me?" Jess could hear her own words slurring, never mind her friend's.

The eyes slowly tried to focus. "Like you…? You mean a lesbian?"

"Yes, what else would I mean?"

"I'm not sure. I mean in answer to the lesbian question, not what else you would mean."

Jess frowned. "This is getting complicated."

"Why?" Julie returned.

"Why what?" Jess sniggered.

Julie frowned. "I don't know. I think I've lost the thread of this. Rachel…"

A man interrupted. "Hello you two, it's great to see you both." They both stood and smiled enthusiastically. "Hi Charlie."

***

It was almost midnight and the two of them stood chatting with a small group of old school friends. Julie suddenly elbowed Jess in the ribs. She nodded toward the door. "It's Maddie."

The small group looked on as the named woman was instantly welcomed by a number of people, almost all of them male.

They heard someone hiss, "Trust her to turn up at this time. Only a grand entrance for that one."

Jess chuckled as she heard Susan from the group say, "Women beware. Those fools have no chance now."

The group laughed as Susan touched Jess's arm. "No offense intended. I'm still holding a grudge against her for stealing my boyfriend at the age of fourteen." The group laughed again.

Susan had been a lifesaver in school. She had guessed Jess's sexual orientation way before even Jess really understood the odd feelings she was having. Her older sister had attended a college for girls and had relayed a number of stories and then advice when Susan had questioned her more closely. Susan initially had approached Julie with her suspicion, who then spoke to Jess. The two of them had then been Jess's support throughout her teenage years and beyond.

"Oh no, here she comes and she is looking right at you, Jess," Charlie said with a wink.

"Hello everyone, how are you all?" Maddie swooped among them with hugs and kisses and saved Jess until the last.

Jess held out her hand in the vain hope of keeping Maddie at bay. She had already managed to alienate her from the rest of the group. It worked. *Amazing.*

"Jess, how are you? Long time no see." She looked her up and down. "The years have been very good to you."

Jess inwardly groaned. "I'm fine, thank you Maddie, and you're looking good yourself." Instantly she cringed. *Why on earth did I say that?* Maddie had always been everyone's dream, men and women alike.

"Oh, thank you. Definitely not as good as you though."

Jess could see Richard, Susan's husband, wiggling his eyebrows over Maddie's shoulder.

The small group had decided that Maddie had no intention of involving them in the conversation and that Jess was more than capable of taking care of herself, so they wandered to the dance floor. Suddenly she was engulfed in a hug. "I was sorry to hear about Jack." *Damn.*

***

Jess soon found herself cornered by Maddie and the two other women from earlier. She seemed totally incapable of extricating herself from them, despite having no interest in any one of them. She gave Julie a pleading look as her friend danced with Charlie. She didn't care that the two of them shared a laugh at her expense before Julie started toward her.

Julie grabbed Jess's hand. "Excuse me ladies, I'm whisking this lovely lady away for a dance." Once they were safely on the dance floor, Julie patted Jess's cheek. "Poor thing, can't you look after yourself anymore?"

"Very funny. I'm being polite, it's a family party."

Julie looked over at the three women. "I don't understand why they haven't asked you to dance. They couldn't get much closer than this." Julie grabbed Jess around the waist, waltzing her around until they both felt a little giddy and had to part.

Jess shouted into Julie's ear. "Believe me they've tried, but I have no intention of flaunting my sexuality here. They aren't exactly being discreet."

Julie, nodded in agreement as they both looked over to the threesome. All eyes were on Jess.

Jess sighed. Three eligible women. *When did the potential for a night of sex get so complicated?* She knew if she left with one of them, she'd be paraded around like a trophy. *Who wants that?*

"Julie if you don't mind I'm going to say my goodbyes and head over to the hotel. Will you wait and get a lift with Susan and Richard?"

"I'll come just now if you like?"

"No, honestly if you're enjoying yourself, stay, I'll be fine."

"Are you sure?"

"Yes, but please don't forget to go with Susan and Richard."

Julie smiled and pecked Jess on the cheek. "I won't Mom."

CHAPTER SIX

Jess walked up to the reception desk of the Mackinlay Hotel. This was her regular place to stay in town. After a record three propositions for a night of pleasure, she'd finally escaped the party alone. "Hi Jane, how are you?" She was pleased to see a familiar face and friend.

"Well hello, Jess. It's been a long time." Once they had exchanged stories and she had caught up on the local gossip she headed up to her room.

Punching her pillows to make herself comfortable, she failed in settling her feeling of frustration at having no company. She needed a cure for her growing infatuation with Rachel, but none of the women available this evening appealed at all and even if they had, it would have been far too complicated.

She smiled in an attempt to relax herself. Was she getting fussy in her old age? Meeting any one of them at anything other than a birthday bash, there would have been no hesitation, she was sure. *I wonder if Maddie would have lived up to expectation?* She chuckled before rolling over and falling into a fitful asleep.

***

Jess woke to gentle knocking at the door. She raised her head sleepily from the pillow and saw Rachel standing at the foot of the bed. She was adorned in an extremely flimsy nightdress that tantalizingly stopped at the top of shapely bronzed legs. Instantly she reached up and pulled her down. Miraculously all their clothing was lost and their bodies pressed urgently together. Jess was beside herself with arousal and all Rachel did was rap her knuckles on her head and whisper repeatedly, "Jess, are you awake? Jess, are you awake?"

"For goodness sake." She opened her eyes wanting desperately to devour Rachel's mouth and silence her ridiculous words. She heard the knocking again and realizing it was someone at the door, stumbled out of bed toward it. *How much did I have to drink?* Opening it she expected to see Julie.

"Hi Jess, can I come in?" Bea looked up and down the corridor before pushing past her. "Sorry, I don't want to be caught going into a guest's room. It wouldn't look too good."

Jess started coming to her senses, although her mouth felt like a cesspit and her libido was playing up badly. "Bea, what are you doing here?"

"I work here, remember? Jane gave me a call and told me you were alone." She raised an eyebrow. "Do you need some company?"

Jess looked at the bedside cabinet. "What time is it?"

"When did time start to matter?" She looked Jess up and down. "Sexy pajamas."

Jess smiled. "I think Julie is next door."

Bea looked a little sheepish. "Ah, she's actually a little further down the corridor now."

Jess chuckled, not able to help it. "I see. Wait here, let me get a drink of water and clean my teeth."

"That sounds promising."

"Don't count your chickens." Jess disappeared into the bathroom.

She had known Bea for ten years and there were ten years between them in age. She'd picked her up one evening in a bar when the cocky, drunken youngster was in danger of ending the night with a number of undesirable women. The belligerent young woman had insisted on sex, or she would go elsewhere. So Jess had obliged, taking a long gentle time over it. The young woman had then cried herself to sleep in Jess's arms. They'd hooked up again, half a dozen times or so over the years, with many a satisfying result. She looked at herself in the mirror as she dried her mouth. *Just what I need.*

As she stepped back into the room, Bea closed the gap and lowered her gaze to lips that were slightly parted. "That look says you could do with some company."

Jess waited for the kiss she knew would come, then pulled away and said, to her own bewilderment, "No, not tonight."

Bea smiled cheekily. "Are you sure about that? I could definitely do with it myself."

She sighed. "Quite sure."

Bea looked at her with want in her eyes and was positive need was reflected straight back. "Okay, but I'm not convinced." At the door she turned around, a frown knitting her eyebrows. "Is everything all right?"

Jess remained rigid and fixed to the spot. She sighed again. "I'd have someone else on my mind."

Bea couldn't help herself, her mouth gaped open and then she blurted, almost laughing, "You!"

Jess rolled her eyes. "It's temporary."

"Well then, maybe I could return a favor. Josie, remember? You helped me erase her image when I couldn't think of entertaining anyone else." Bea had been devastated when her lover of five years had left her. "I'm not promising it will be as effective, but you never know."

Closing the gap between them, with more purpose this time, she cupped the back of Jess's head and pulled her lips hard to her own. Urgency bubbled almost immediately in them both. Jess swiftly removed Bea's clothing and eased her back onto the bed. Jess smiled to herself. *Easy clothes to take off, she came prepared.* Straddling the body beneath her, she looked into a face full of desire.

Bea pulled Jess down by her T-shirt and covered her lips again, tongues danced in and out, fighting for supremacy. Legs wrapped around Jess's waist and wet swollen folds pressed hard against her palm and abdomen. Bea sucked in a breath when fingers began to tease her clitoris; she was so close. Pushing harder, she gasped, "Three please, make it three." As she shifted her position the fingers slipped inside. "Oh yes, Jess, yes." They both rocked in unison, pushing harder against one another until Bea's cry of release was stifled by a mouth-devouring kiss.

***

Jess woke to darkness, still dressed in her nightwear, and alone. Usually it was she who crept out of bed first. Sitting up, she shook her head. "Amazing. No headache." Noticing a shard of light coming from under the bathroom door, she propped herself up and waited. The door opened and Bea stood dressed and ready to go.

She smirked. "Good morning and where do you think you're going?"

Bea switched off the light and put on the bedroom dimmer. "To work, unfortunately, or else I'd be back in that bed in a flash."

Jess got up and wrapped her arms around Bea's waist. "How long have you got?"

"Not long enough."

"Oh, I'm sure we could make it quick." Jess whispered mischievously, sliding her hands into Bea's trousers and massaging her buttocks. Jess was aroused, and she could tell from the heat rising in Bea's body that it would take little effort to make her come.

The younger woman moaned, burying her head in Jess's neck. "How quick?"

Jess pulled back and started guiding her back toward the bed. "I'll show you."

***

Bea started dressing again. "I hope I substituted well enough for the woman you were talking about?"

Jess frowned, suddenly feeling self-conscious and a little callous toward both women. She hadn't given Rachel a thought. "Yes, actually, I never thought of her at all."

Bea snorted. "I knew it was too good to be true."

Jess raised an eyebrow. "What?"

"You, being hung up on somebody."

Jess couldn't understand why she felt uncomfortable, so she cruelly changed the subject. "Who is Lilly?"

Bea stopped suddenly, almost tripping in her attempt to put a leg into her joggers and stared at Jess. "My God I didn't? Please don't say I did? I wasn't thinking of her at all, I was incapable."

Jess chuckled at the mortified look. "Sorry, I'm being evil. You mentioned her in your sleep."

"I don't believe it. I'm sorry." She smirked. "It was definitely you who was giving me the time of my life, no one else."

"I'm sorry too. As I said, I was being wicked. You don't need to explain."

The smile went as the younger woman slumped down on the bed next to her. "Oh damn it. I have a thing about her and it's really doing my head in. She's a wonderful woman and with a total jerk who treats her like dirt. I'm waiting for her to wake up to that fact." She sighed. "She's not rushing herself though."

Jess placed a hand on the knee next to hers. "Maybe she has a certain opinion about you and your lifestyle. Sometimes, it's better the devil you know."

Bea sniggered. "That's why I was in last night. Friday nights are a rare night off and not usually ones to stay at home. I'm trying to stay away from the scene a little, or at least if I'm at the bar I'm not leaving with anyone. I'm not sure this celibacy lark is going to pay off though, so you were my safe bet and boy did I need one."

Jess chuckled to herself. This woman knew her too well. If she had said that to anyone else, she'd be on her backside on the other side of the door by now.

Bea stood. "Lilly's partner is the DJ at Roxy's."

Jess raised her eyebrows. "You mean…?"

"Don't. She's lovely, and that bruiser of a girlfriend is a bully."

Jess frowned. "What do you mean, a bully? I thought she was just a pain in the proverbial?"

"Oh, not in the physical sense. She likes to play mind games. She's always putting Lilly down and certainly doesn't like her speaking to many people."

Jess stood and took Bea's hand. "That can be just as bad as any physical abuse. Keep talking to her, I'm sure she appreciates it."

Bea smiled conspiratorially. "Yes, I think she does, and I'm pretty sure my patience will be rewarded eventually."

"Good, I hope it is, but be careful."

Bea slipped on her trainers. "She's all show. You know that. Anyway, what about you?"

Jess asked, puzzled, "What about me?"

"Your fantasy woman."

She laughed. "No such thing. I just haven't had a good night out in a quite a while. That's all. Gorgeous women are few and far between in my neck of the woods and when one appears, well…"

"Gorgeous, you say?"

Jess put her hands on Bea's shoulders, turned her around toward the door and smacked her bottom. "I thought you were late for work?"

"I'm going. Good to see you, Jess. Maybe see you around. And thanks." Bea smiled as she went out the door, after quickly looking up and down the corridor.

Jess returned to her bed. There was another three hours before she was to meet Julie for breakfast. Rachel popped into her head again as she pulled the covers up and lay her head on the pillow.

She laughed. What was it about that woman? *She's haunting me.* She had to concede, she was attractive, but far too genteel for a night of no strings attached sex. Jess imagined she would be someone who liked it slow, teasing and sensuous, building to a sweet crescendo. She wondered if Rachel's head would thrash from side to side as her body craved release. *Good grief, what are you doing to yourself?* Suddenly aware of a warm, moist throb, her hand slid beneath the sheets and into her pajamas before she fell sound asleep.

***

The alarm was piercing. Jess washed, dressed and packed. Quickly glancing at the sheet of hotel paper, on which Bea had written Julie's room number, she headed out and crossed the landing. Julie eventually opened the door after persistent knocking and groaned at the cheerful figure standing in her doorway. Jess winked at a very fragile looking person. "Morning, are you ready for breakfast?" All she received was a dismissive look.

Jess enjoyed a breakfast of cereal, eggs, bacon and toast, washed down with orange juice and tea. All Julie could manage was a half slice of dry toast with her coffee, and that was a struggle. Once finished, they headed to reception to hand in their keys and store their bags until Mark and Rose picked them up later in the day.

"Hello Julie, how are you?" She looked up to see Bea smiling, before giving Jess a very quick glance.

Julie looked at Jess, who was looking at Bea with a grin. She turned to Bea and unconvincingly answered, "Fine thanks. How are you?"

Chuckling, Bea replied, "Good, thank you. Enjoyed the céilidh then?"

"Yes. But this morning, no."

As they stepped out onto the street, Julie looked at her friend. "You didn't spend the night alone, did you?"

Jess immediately blushed before answering coyly, "Maybe not."

"I don't think there's a maybe about it. You couldn't act the innocent, even if you were."

Jess feigned hurt. "That's not nice."

"I'm not trying to be nice. How can you two do it? I mean, have sex regularly and just walk away?"

Jess frowned at the brusque tone. She knew where this conversation was going and it definitely wasn't going to be helped by Julie's hangover. "For one, it's not regular and for another, it will hopefully be the last."

"What do you mean by the last?"

"She has her sights set on someone."

Julie gaped at her and screeched, "And she's sleeping with you? God help them."

Jess glared at her friend who was holding her head and looking extremely pale. "Listen Julie, Bea is probably one of the most loyal people I know. She just wants to love someone who will love her back and live happily ever after. So don't judge her."

Julie spoke more carefully, ignoring Jess's tone. "And you're not that person?"

"No, I am not and wouldn't even pretend to be. She deserves much better than me. Anyway, this person she's interested in is not available yet, so I think she has every right to satisfy her need with a trustworthy source."

Julie wasn't in the mood for a fight and Jess didn't deserve her judgment. "You're a real softie, you know, and whether you like it or not, you do care, and she couldn't possibly deserve a better friend than she already has. I'm sorry." She linked her arm through Jess's.

Jess couldn't believe she'd got away so lightly. "Um well, from what she said, I have no doubt she'll get what she wants. I hope so, anyway."

CHAPTER SEVEN

"Uncle Jack, are you out the back?"

"Yes."

Jess opened a cupboard door. "Would you like a ginger beer, or tea and hunk of cake?"

"We've got it all out here, come and join us."

Jess walked through to the conservatory. "Who's we? Oh, Rachel." She beamed and added a little too enthusiastically, "Great to see you. How are you?" Attempting to curb her excitement at seeing this woman, she turned and settled into the chair next to her uncle.

Rachel smiled from the chair opposite. "I'm fine thank you, and it's good to see you too."

Jess smiled back. Slowly directing her attention to her uncle she asked, "More tea, or cake?"

Both of them were grinning at her now. "No thank you."

Taking a deep breath she helped herself and then took a furtive glance Rachel's way. "How did the book meeting go? Or have you been through that already?"

Much to Jess's relief, this began a relaxed conversation; the initial nervousness they all exhibited when she came in dwindled.

Rachel recounted her trip to Edinburgh and the unexpected three-day extension due to thrashing out deadlines. She'd spent an enjoyable time showing her two friends from London, Margaret and Diane, around the city. "Diane couldn't believe the Royal Mile was only a mile long. It took us a day and a half to complete."

Jess laughed. "You must have visited every tourist attraction along its route or was that just the shops?" Fresh tea was dispensed and Jess found herself drifting as Rachel continued excitedly about cobbled streets, stone tenement buildings, the Jacobite rising and Mary Queen of Scots. She sank back into the chair vaguely aware of the voices.

Her gaze was drawn to Rachel. She looked happy, obviously enjoying playing guide to her friends, and as always she looked immaculate. There never seemed to be a thing out of place, not even a hair. Her clothes and accessories were all color coordinated, her makeup, although subtle, was the right shade to enhance those beautiful dark eyes. And those lips, those soft rosy, luscious lips…

"Jess? Are you with us, Jess?" Suddenly aware of a hand on her arm and Uncle Jack's voice, she started, splashing tea everywhere on the table before hurriedly putting the cup down with a thump. She quickly began wiping the mess up with a handy tea towel and squeaked, "Sorry." Then cleared her throat. "My apologies, that was rude. I must have drifted off."

She looked at Rachel and could feel the heat of a blush rising. *Please not so obvious.*

"I know when I've bored someone into submission," Rachel quipped.

Jack laughed.

"No," Jess said anxiously, "You didn't bore me, I…" She gave up and picked up her cup as the two of them began to laugh at her again. The heat of her blush was beginning to make her perspire. "Damn." She slumped back into the chair, spilling more tea, which led to more laughter.

***

Rachel wedged the telephone between her ear and shoulder and carried her glass of wine over to the sofa. "I just can't work her out Margaret. I am absolutely certain she's a lesbian but… Oh, I don't know, maybe she isn't."

"You're not just focusing on the issue of whether she is gay or not, with the hope she may fancy you?"

"No I'm not," Rachel retorted.

Margaret chuckled. "Okay, I was just wondering. You've mentioned her more than any other woman, besides Michelle, of course. You'd only known her for about a month before Edinburgh and her name came up an awful lot."

Rachel paused. She wasn't quite sure how to respond. Yes, she liked Jess. In fact, her thoughts were becoming more sexual in nature.

Apparently uneasy at the silence, her friend said, "Sorry Rach, have I put my foot in it?"

She chuckled. "No you haven't." She sighed. "I think you may well be right."

"Why, the sigh then? That's great. You deserve a little fun and happiness with what sounds like an adorable woman."

"If I'm this confused about her, she couldn't possibly be that interested."

"How do you know she isn't? You don't even know if she's gay."

"That's what I mean. If she were, surely I would know."

Margaret softened her tone. "Not if you're afraid of disappointment, or rejection."

Rachel sighed, defeated. "I'm probably best not knowing. My last two attempts with woman were pitiful. In fact, my whole relationship track record is a disgrace."

"I set you up with the last two remember? It was my poor judgment and you handled yourself perfectly. You weren't exactly interested, remember? Jess you've found all on your own. Find out her orientation and if it's positive, have some fun. What have you got to lose?"

"My summer home and my reputation. I don't want to upset anyone here for nothing."

"You're far too serious for your own good. How disastrous could it really be? Maybe the reason she's giving out mixed signals is that she is not sure of you. You're a very good income to them, remember?"

Rachel exclaimed, "Margaret that is awful!"

"Well, it's true."

"I suppose there could be some element of truth in that." She sighed. "The way she looks at me sometimes, I could swear it's pure...oh I don't know."

"Desire? I think you mentioned earlier."

She laughed. "I did, didn't I? The only problem is when I feel I see it, she puts up some sort of barrier. Am I sounding desperate?" Margaret chuckled as she continued. "I don't want to make a fool of myself. I've done that once and I don't intend ever doing it again." Bitterness rising, she thought of Michelle. "No way is anyone going to do that to me again."

Margaret interrupted her gently. "Rachel, not everyone is Michelle. You know that."

She took a calming breath. "You're right, I'm sorry." Michelle had been her partner for thirteen years. It had been good between them in the beginning, or so she thought. Looking back on it, Rachel was unsure exactly for how long she had deluded herself. Life had always revolved around Michelle and what she wanted. There had been affairs and not just the two Rachel knew of. It still hurt when she thought of the life they had shared, the one she'd foolishly fought so hard to keep. Going over and over, dissecting every aspect with a therapist, the only conclusion she had ever reached was that she had thrown away thirteen years of her life.

"Just be yourself," Margaret advised her. "You are a lovely person and despite what you may think, quite a catch for anyone, believe me."

"Thank you Margaret, you're a good friend."

"Ask her more personal questions, stop beating around the bush."

Rachel laughed. "You're right. I'm tying myself in knots, when it should be so simple. I get the impression Jess is reasonably open and honest. I'm probably just making it difficult for us both."

Margaret said, "That's the spirit. Go find out, girl."

CHAPTER EIGHT

Jess and Julie were settling down at either end of the oversized sofa. Julie began to massage Jess's foot. They were enjoying one of their girlie nights, as they called them. Tom was away for the night, all expenses paid by a drug company attempting to recruit doctors and their patients into a clinical trial.

Laughing, Jess almost choked on her wine. "I can't believe Maddie managed to have sex with Lee and then leave with Karen. No wonder the family is upset and embarrassed. I can imagine Harriet Simpson's shock." She attempted to mimic Maddie's mother: "Even that Brewster girl wouldn't stoop so low, Maddie. You're a disgrace."

Julie started to laugh as well, before growing annoyed. "I just don't know where they get their information about you. Your reputation is a hundred times worse than the reality. How does that happen? They don't know you at all."

Jess smiled ruefully. "A hundred times, that's not bad. If only it were true, I'd be having a whale of a time." She laughed as Julie squeezed her toes. "Don't let it upset you. The people who matter the most know me better than that."

Julie attempted a smile, a rather half-hearted effort, so her foot received a tickle. She giggled and pulled it away, then slid it back into place.

Jess added, "The adults in that family never really liked me anyway. I was too fond of their daughter and not of their son."

Julie nodded and sniggered. Her irritation began to rise again. "Maddie was never discreet with her men. It's funny, that just because her preferences change, it's a disgrace to be so wanton."

Jess grinned. Her friend always defended the fact she was seen as different. She didn't tolerate people's perceptions that some things were acceptable for heterosexuals and not for homosexuals. She wanted to lighten her friend's mood. "You know I don't remember hearing of Maddie having two men in one night though. Consecutive nights maybe." They both tittered as they took a sip of wine.

Suddenly Jess grimaced in remembrance and Julie pinched her toe. "What?"

"Actually I do know of one night. I remembered wondering at the time what I ever saw in her."

Julie snorted loudly. "The same as the boys. Blond hair, big boobs and a very suggestive smile. I never took your crush on her too seriously. I'm not sure you did either."

Jess smirked. "You're probably right. If she'd shown any interest, I'd have been petrified and run the other way." *Would you though, given the chance? Thank goodness I never had a choice.*

Julie sat forward, the wine definitely giving her a buzz. "Explain the one night. I can't believe you haven't told me this before."

Jess hesitated, realizing why she hadn't mentioned it. "It was at the sixth form party."

"Ah." Julie squeezed her foot. "Go on, you can't stop now."

Jess relaxed. "Well, I saw Maddie in three compromising positions that night, with three different boys."

Julie gasped. "You've got to be kidding?"

"I don't know why I'm finding this funny. Just the thought of it…" She scrunched up her face. "If I hadn't known I was different from the rest of you, it certainly wouldn't have taken much to sway me after that."

Julie laughed. "Hetero sex, not a pretty sight for you then?" She rubbed her hands together.

Jess described the drunken night, where a whole bunch of teenagers were allowed to celebrate end of school, unsupervised. Neither of them could believe the goings-on, as they exchanged memories. Jess finally said, "She was actually saying, that's enough I can't do this again." There was a pause before she quietly added, "That's when I heard you."

She glanced at Julie and gently stroked her foot. They were silent for a moment until Julie whispered, "Thank you."

That night Jess had been the only one whose hormones weren't on the rampage. Her uncle had warned her not to drink and to keep an eye on her friends. And as she always did, she did as she was told. She was grateful to him though, or she may not have been able to save Julie from Damien Hall. A boy Julie didn't even particularly like. Yes, she had flirted with him, kissed and cuddled, curious where it might lead. Then when he started undoing his trousers and grappled with Julie's jeans, she had asked him to stop. That hadn't deterred him and she was powerless. She was drunk and felt she'd encouraged him. Trying to reason with him was futile and as the horror of what was to come grew, she pleaded desperately again. Jess had heard her cries and yanked him off before he managed to penetrate her. Jess, the girl who was different, had then taken the jeers of wanting to keep Julie for herself, as she hurriedly helped her friend to dress, keeping all the others at bay, and in particular, a raging Damien. Ironically, most of Jess's peers now admired and respected her. With life's experience they had all matured in their beliefs; the people that mattered, anyway.

They were both wrapped up in their own thoughts for a while before Julie asked. "More wine?"

Jess looked over at her. "Not if it's going to make you morose?"

Julie rose and kissed the top of Jess's head. "No, that night made me save myself for much better men. And I couldn't have found a better one than Tom." She sat after filling their glasses. "I haven't asked you about Rachel and her trip to Edinburgh."

Jess blushed at the rush of feeling that washed over her at the mention of the gorgeous brunette's name.

Julie raised her eyebrows at the response. "Is there something I should know?"

"No. Of course not," Jess grumped, and stomped over to the fireplace, turning her back on the room.

"What have I said?"

Jess glanced back at her friend and sighed. "Oh nothing. I'm sorry. I just thought...nothing." Her behavior was becoming increasingly uncharacteristic over Rachel. Rarely had her feelings strayed past pleasure and friendship in the past because when they did, disaster always struck. That's all she had to remember, it wasn't difficult. *You're just being ridiculous.* "She's a bit of puzzlement to me."

"Why?"

Jess sighed. "I can't work out whether she's gay or straight and for some weird reason, it's bothering me." Julie said nothing. She chuckled nervously. "I just hope for everyone's sake she's straight."

Julie attempted not to sound too excited. "Why is that so important?"

Jess noted the tone, but chose to ignore it this time. "If I knew for certain she was straight, I could stop thinking about..."

"What? What would you then stop thinking about?"

Jess reddened and flopped herself back on the sofa. "I'm like a dog in heat! The only thing that's keeping me in check is the thought she might be straight." Julie couldn't help it, she had to laugh. "It's not funny," Jess protested. "It's driving me mad."

"All right. What if she isn't straight and available? Why can't you satisfy your desires and see where it leads?"

"If I'd met her in a bar, it would have been perfect. We'd have had a wonderful night together and that would have been that. As it is, it would be a horrendous mistake." She looked directly at Julie. "She has been coming here for years and loves it. What right do I have to spoil that, just to indulge some pathetic need of mine?"

"You obviously think a lot of her to be getting yourself so worked up."

Jess narrowed her eyes and asked suspiciously, "What are you trying to say?"

"It's plain, you care for her."

"For heaven's sake, I know where you're heading, Julie. You've known Rachel for six years and not once have you suggested I stay a summer and check her out. It was Maddie a couple of weeks ago. And if she's straight..." She shook her head. "What is your problem?" *I know what my problem is. I don't think she's straight at all.*

Julie frowned. "Is wanting your friend to be happy and not alone a problem?"

"How many times do I have to tell you, I am not unhappy and I am not alone?"

Julie sighed. "I've never known you to get yourself in a pickle over something you can't have. You simply walk away, just like you did when you first met her."

Jess closed her eyes, not wanting to argue. "She is totally off limits and it's due to that fact, I've become obsessed, that's all."

"Then what are you going to do?"

"Nothing. Admire her from a distance and satisfy my libido elsewhere." That was another problem. Her night of noncommittal sex after a grueling seven months of work and stress only led to her feeling like she had betrayed Rachel. *Totally irrational.*

"That's cold. What if she has feelings for you?"

Jess groaned. "Please, she hasn't shown any interest in me, whatsoever."

"So you don't know if she will reciprocate your feelings?"

Jess glared. "Julie, listen to me. That doesn't matter. Even if she would, I am not going there." She attempted to soften her tone. "She means too much to Uncle Jack. I couldn't do that to him. And I couldn't do it to her. She would end up hurt. Nothing is worth any of that."

"Jess, you're just afraid. I think you've found someone who's more than a passing fancy and you're fighting it. You cannot keep blaming yourself for events that were not your fault. You have to let it go. You're not giving yourself a chance of ever having the joy of sharing your life with someone."

Jess's impatience rose again. "I never said I wanted to spend the rest of my life with the woman. I'm lusting after her, nothing more, nothing less, and I will not be responsible for anyone else's harm." Jess wanted an end to this conversation. "Uncle Jack is due his follow-up tests the day after tomorrow. I need to concentrate on him, nothing else is important."

Julie sighed, sliding her arm around her friend's shoulders and drawing her into a hug. "I know and I want to be here for you. That's what's important to me, I'm sorry."

CHAPTER NINE

After arriving back from taking her Uncle Jack and Marie down to the village, Jess started work on replacing a long section of unstable fencing that bordered the estate. The task was huge, and her mood was lifted when Rachel appeared late in the morning and insisted on helping. Rachel actually slowed her progress, but she didn't care, the company and the eagerness of her assistant was a pleasant distraction from thinking about her uncle. The tests he'd had were neither encouraging or discouraging. The cancer hadn't appeared to have spread, yet they'd hoped to have seen a little more progress in his health.

Rachel looked up as she put her last post in place as instructed. "Jess, this may seem like a stupid question, but where did you learn all these practical skills? Is it just experience?"

Jess put her mattock down and examined the hole for size. "Yes, mostly from Uncle Jack, he was builder and did a bit of everything. Oh, I did go on a short electrical course."

"Electrical?"

"Yes. Our guests could probably survive most botched jobs, even a few dodgy roof tiles, but electrocution. That wouldn't be good."

Rachel tut-tutted, "I don't believe you do any of your jobs badly." She grinned. "Your uncle wouldn't let you."

Jess laughed, picking up a post and placing it in the hole. "You're right there."

"Have you been to college or university at all?"

Jess smiled. "Could you hold this please? Not university. I did go to college for a business diploma. It was only for a year. I thought it might be helpful. And, all my orienteering I have done through college to gain my certification."

"For the walking holidays?"

"Yes and…Just tilt that a wee bit toward me." Jess chuckled. "And don't grip it quite so tightly."

Rachel slackened her hold on the post and watched as Jess swung the mallet. Every muscle was emphasized with the motion and the smooth pale area of her belly that peeped out on each swing was mesmerizing.

"Rachel, you can let go."

She blinked. "Sorry. I was miles away. The walking company, what exactly is it you do? Besides walk?" Rachel inwardly rolled her eyes.

Jess wasn't entirely sure what Rachel was staring at but she was sure she was admiring something. That wasn't helping Jess, especially as it was giving her a very pleasant feeling in the area of her body she was desperately trying to ignore. "I go away with groups. Sometimes it's a long-distance trek, others can be daily walks in one particular area, or I do specialist ones, looking at local flora and fauna. The holidays are mostly in Britain and in some parts of Europe."

"So, do you cover Scotland?"

"Occasionally. I'm a little more flexible than most, so it varies."

"Why do you do it?"

Jess smiled. "I enjoy it. Uncle Jack thought I should do something other than work here. Meet new people, that sort of thing. Last year was my tenth anniversary." Jess didn't like to think it would be the last. And that wasn't because she thought she would miss it.

"Well, before I ask you another silly question, I don't know about you, but I'm hungry. I'm going to go and get us some lunch. You'll have to carry on without my valuable assistance." Rachel grinned.

"You really don't have to do that."

"I know, but it seems a shame not to make the most of a beautiful day. There is still a lot of work to be done."

Jess looked at the timber still stacked. "We won't finish that today." She laughed at Rachel's knowing look. "Sorry."

"I'll be back shortly."

When Rachel returned they discussed the plan for the afternoon and then quietly tucked into their sandwiches. Jess glanced over at Rachel thinking how easy she was to talk to. This would be an ideal time to talk privately and stop any future problems arising, if they were ever going to. Suddenly she felt nervous.

She coughed, attempting to clear the tightness that was taking control of her throat and then asked, "Rachel, have you ever married?"

"No," came a somewhat wary reply.

"How about a partner then?"

Rachel looked up, making eye contact, and nodded. "Yes."

Jess anxiously wiped the palms of her hands on her trousers before grasping her mug to steady them. "I'm sorry. I didn't mean to pry, forget I asked."

Rachel gave her a faint smile. "We separated just over six years ago. We were together for thirteen years."

"Thirteen? That's amazing."

"Yes it is." Rachel couldn't help sounding bitter and quickly reined herself in. "What about you, any partners or long-term relationships?"

Jess began to fidget and bit her bottom lip. "Umm, no, not really."

"None?"

"Well, I did have one relationship that lasted around five, maybe six months."

Rachel's eyes widened. "Is that the only one?"

"Um, yes." Jess paused; the face looking at her showed light-hearted horror. She began to relax. "I might also be stretching the meaning of the word *relationship* a little."

"I see. So if your relationships have been limited, what about sexual liaisons then? If that isn't too personal?" A mischievous grin suddenly appeared. "If I tell you how many I've had, will you tell me how many you've had?"

Jess couldn't help but laugh. "Go on then, how many?"

"I could just about count them on one hand."

Jess feigned shock. "One hand?"

"Yes, how about you?"

Jess raised an eyebrow, inspecting her hand. "It would have to be an extremely deformed hand to count mine on the one."

Rachel chuckled. "I see. So how long do these sexual liaisons of yours last?"

With a wicked smile she said, "All night, if the person I'm with has any stamina."

"Good grief, Jess. I meant the average number of days, weeks or months with the same—individual."

"Oh." Jess quickly tried to judge how Rachel was taking this information. She didn't appear too disgusted. Rachel was monogamous and from her experience they never really trusted those who had many lovers. "Well around twelve hours, tops."

"You weren't joking then!"

Jess thought maybe she had gone a little too far. She didn't particularly want Rachel to think she was some sort of brazen hussy. "It could be the same person on different occasions."

Rachel just looked at her, mouth agape. She gave Rachel what she thought was a pleading look. "If it's any consolation, I was a late starter and probably felt I had to make up for lost time."

"How late?"

"Twenty-four. Actually not far off twenty-five."

"Well I'll be. I thought I was late at nineteen. What took you so long?"

She replied cautiously. "There isn't a great deal of opportunity around here. How about you?"

"There was much more opportunity when I went to the College of Art." She narrowed her eyes at Jess. "I always thought farmers' sons were more than happy to take a young girl's flower?" She batted her eyelids.

Jess laughed. "Flower, my God, I haven't heard that term in years." She looked seriously at Rachel. "You're right. There were plenty of boys more than willing, but no…" Jess stopped. "Next to no girls. What's your excuse?"

Rachel nodded. There was something more in that pause of Jess's. "The same. College was much more liberating." She smiled at Jess, "I had guessed, well I was ninety-nine point nine percent certain."

Jess raised a querying eyebrow. "Really? I have to say I was pretty sure too. I mean about you. But it's not something you go around asking." She grinned. "And I have been known to get it wrong. Not good."

Rachel laughed and shook her head. She looked at Jess. "You don't have to answer this, but can I ask you something?"

"Yes," Jess replied a little cautiously.

"You said—next to no girls." Rachel again saw that distant, even sad look. But as before, it was fleeting.

Jess smiled softly. "Her name was Kirsty. I suppose it is like many stories. We were fourteen and unaware until then that you could be attracted to another girl instead of a boy. We'd known each other since kindergarten." Jess chuckled. "The term lesbian I hadn't even heard of, until Julie mentioned it afterward." Jess smiled again. "Neither of us knew what to do about being in lust with another girl. It never went very far." Jess remembered their few kisses and a little fumbling, then their embarrassed looks.

"Was she your first love then?"

"Yes and the last."

"Oh."

Jess chuckled at Rachel's expression. "It's not how it sounds. I'm not pining with a broken heart, if that's what you're thinking." Jess suddenly felt anxious.

"What happened?"

"Um. I'm afraid she died."

"Oh, Jess, I'm sorry."

"Don't be. You can be for Kirsty, but not for me. It was a long time ago."

"Still, it can't be easy." Rachel thought of Jess's family.

"Actually, I dread to think where she might be now, if she had lived. She knew how to live life then."

"So you don't think it would have lasted?" Rachel smiled. Jess was obviously trying to stop any gloom arising.

"No. I might have got started earlier, but she would have soon gone on to pastures new. Even then, Kirsty wasn't planning on staying around here."

"And you were?"

"I couldn't imagine living anywhere else. Why would I? Everything I want and enjoy out of life is here."

Rachel couldn't argue with that, she couldn't see Jess anywhere else either. She sighed.

"So, a long-term relationship, is that something that has just eluded you, or is it because you don't want one?"

Jess sucked in a breath, she'd been given a reminder, and now a lifeline had been thrown. She had to make her position clear. Then without warning her mind betrayed her, conjuring up an image of closing the gap and easing Rachel to the ground and taking her slowly, over and over again. The heat rose so quickly throughout her body, she shook her head in an attempt to divert the throb that was settling at her center. Sighing heavily she said what she wanted to say. "No I have never wanted one and I can't see that ever changing."

Rachel saw a multitude of emotions cross the face in front of her; apprehension, annoyance, resignation and unmistakably desire. She'd hoped that maybe Jess just hadn't found the right person and at that moment in time, she felt it could easily have been her. The reply when it came was such a disappointment, not what she was expecting. She couldn't believe her reaction to the admission either—she was too old to waste any more time on playgirls. Rachel was a master at masking her feelings. Something she had perfected over the years. "Well Jess, you're honest if nothing else." She attempted a relaxed smile and then laughed. "I wouldn't want to lose my second home for some sort of short-term pleasure, so I think we're both safe."

They worked quietly for the rest of the afternoon. Jess wasn't quite sure how to take what Rachel had said. Convincing herself she'd upset this very likable woman's feelings, she couldn't keep quiet any longer. "Rachel, I'm sorry if what I said earlier appeared conceited. I happen to like you and enjoy the times we spend together. If our relationship went any further than friends, I would end up hurting you, and I don't want to do that." She sighed at the seriousness on Rachel's face, unable to determine the emotion behind it. She attempted a more jovial tone. "Oh and another thing, Uncle Jack would murder me if I drove you out of his life. Could we be friends? Good friends?"

Rachel had to laugh, that blush was just so adorable. She couldn't deny fantasizing about Jess and hoping Jess would find her irresistible. She was well aware that she herself was an attractive woman. Those gorgeous blue eyes had definitely made it clear they were aware of it too. The strong athletic woman before her was sexually experienced. Rachel had very rarely enjoyed sex. It had been fun in her early years but with Michelle... Michelle had regularly made comments as to what a lousy lover she was. Rachel had desperately made attempts to improve her performance and somewhere along the line had learnt at least how to pleasure Michelle. She on the other hand, received no real enjoyment and on many occasions had faked an orgasm, all to keep Michelle happy and avoid the..."You really are hopeless. You don't know how to enjoy yourself, Rachel. Relax."

Pulling herself out of her depressing reverie, she looked at Jess. "Friends is fine with me, I couldn't cope with anything more. So good friends is perfect."

Jess said, "Friends then," and stuck out her hand.

"Friends," came the reply, as they shook on it.

CHAPTER TEN

The next couple of months flew by. The summer was proving to be just as busy as the winter. The disc in Don's back had to be surgically removed so he had been of little help around the estate, for which he felt guilty. Jean constantly worried he would try to do too much and not be fit to emigrate. Jack worried over Jess. Jess worried about Jack, and Marie just worried about them all.

This particular day was a bad one for Jess. Her uncle had received the results to further tests and they hadn't been good. The cancer had spread. She had tried to prepare herself for bad news. There had been no real improvement in his energy and fitness levels since the previous ones and his appetite and interest in food had dwindled again.

The only thought that brought a smile to her face, as she sat staring out of her bedroom window, was Rachel. She had been busy with exhibitions, presentations, sketching, painting and meetings. Any free time she had she spent with Uncle Jack or helping Jess where she could. She had proved to be a quick leaner and her enthusiasm was marvelous. They had become the very good friends that Jess had wanted.

Sighing, she stood. Uncle Jack and Marie would be waiting for her. Marie's sobs had echoed through the house at the news, yet she rallied herself quickly and disappeared into the kitchen to prepare afternoon tea for the three of them. At the hospital they had discussed with the consultant the terminal diagnosis. He had offered Jack further radiation to slow things down, but he had refused. In her head she understood his decision. He didn't want to go through all the discomfort again. He wanted to enjoy, as best he could, the time he had left with as much dignity as possible. She fought back the tears again before heading down the stairs. *You're thinking of yourself. Think of him.*

***

Rachel waited in anticipation. Jack had asked her if she would invite Jess to dinner this evening. He knew the trip to the hospital would tire him and he wanted time alone. Jack had confessed to her that he had expected the news not to be good. He knew he was dying. He thought an evening with Rachel would distract Jess, or at least let her talk to someone other than Marie or himself.

Rachel glanced out the window and caught sight of a lost-looking soul plodding up the hill. The redhead she knew always held her head high, commanding the space around her. Not this one. She swallowed down a hard lump forming in her throat. Her tears had spilled over a couple of days ago when Jack had confided in her. She had to be strong for Jess.

She heard the gentle knock at the door, took a deep breath, forced a smile and opened it. "Hi." Rachel had grown used to the way Jess looked at her and was still convinced it was a look of pure desire. She'd often heard people say that Jess could never hide how she was really feeling. Rachel usually enjoyed the look. Tonight though, she had to be mistaken.

As the door opened all Jess wanted to do was bury her unhappiness in exploring every part of this woman. She wanted to see that smile after she had teased, kissed and licked Rachel to orgasm. The thoughts were making her giddy and she felt herself sway. A hand grasped her wrist. "Jess, are you all right?" She couldn't respond. Lights twinkled before her. "Jess, sit down." She was guided urgently to a seat and then her head was suddenly thrust forward. Blackness briefly engulfed her, and then blood began to rush through her ears, followed by more colored lights.

She relaxed at the feel of a hand caressing her back and another high on her thigh. The hand slipped a little further between her legs and full, moist lips were but inches away. But, the eyes she met showed only concern. She desperately attempted to focus on them, to steady her wavering body and mind.

Rachel become conscious of where her hand was resting and slowly withdrew it. In a lighthearted, mocking tone she said, "Well I'm no nurse, but I would say you were close to fainting, my dear." They both laughed, as Jess recovered herself.

Jess relayed the events of the day to Rachel over dinner. She was touched when the big brown beautiful eyes filled with tears. She knew Rachel would be upset; she and Uncle Jack had grown very close over the years.

"I'm sorry, I shouldn't be getting upset, you have more than enough to deal with. I'll just go and get us dessert."

Jess quickly followed. Rachel quietly moved around the kitchen, placing items on a tray. She leaned against the door frame and watched the gentle sway of Rachel's hips, the subtle bounce of round, firm breasts and the teasing way those full pink lips pouted in concentration. All Jess wanted to do was pull that body close to hers and cover those lips with her own. Rachel was a gorgeous woman and you would have to be dead not to notice her. That's what Jess kept telling herself.

Back in the living room they talked for a little while longer before Rachel sensed that was enough for Jess. She suggested Jess stretch out and make herself comfy while she put on a film.

It wasn't long before the curls started to bob and Jess succumbed to sleep. The film was no longer of interest to Rachel either, so she took the opportunity to study the face of the woman who had provided a lot of joy this summer. Jess's features were well defined and strong, yet with a softness to them. The mop of red hair had grown more unruly as the weeks had progressed, but its untamed look complemented its owner perfectly. The sun had most definitely lightened it, giving a lovely golden glow to Jess's face. The twinkling blue eyes were hidden and her lips, fractionally parted, were perfect in their shape. She slowly traced the body relaxed before her. It was so lean, the well-defined muscles held no bulk, yet their strength was apparent. There was no doubting this woman enjoyed the outdoors.

Rachel sighed, contentedly thinking if the muscles in her abdomen were as taut as those elsewhere they would ripple with movement. She instantly wanted to feel those muscles glide over her. To know how those lips would feel against hers. To have those hands cupping and gently caressing her breasts. To feel the strong, long fingers stroke, tease and slide into where she needed them most.

***

"Margaret, I've never been so turned on and she wasn't even touching me. In fact, she wasn't even conscious."

There was a laugh on the other end of the telephone line. "I wish I could have that effect on someone, even Diane for that matter."

"I'm forty-four, for goodness sake, I should be able to show some control. I must be regressing."

"No, I think you mean progressing. I told you right at the beginning to relax and go get the girl, but no, you make friends."

"There's no need to be sarcastic. You're supposed to be my guide in life and provide me with worldly advice."

"Now who's being sarcastic? Listen Rachel, I've never been good at giving you advice when it comes to women. We always fall out."

"No we don't. You quite rightly didn't trust or like Michelle."

"Rachel, I wasn't the one in love with her. Anyway, what about the last two women?"

"You couldn't know what they were really like?"

"I still insisted on setting you up, especially with weird, sexual, foot-fetish woman."

They both laughed. "I don't know, Margaret, one minute I want to rip the clothes off her back, and then the next I'm absolutely petrified at the thought. I honestly wouldn't know what to do with a woman like Jess."

"What do you mean?"

"She knows what she wants and is content."

"You're just a little intimidated by her. You feel she has more experience than you."

"Well, she has."

"Rachel, she may have confessed to no long-term relationships and a number of women. That doesn't automatically mean she's had sex more times than you, just maybe a little more variety. She may well be intimidated with the fact you'd been with one woman for so long."

"You can be crude sometimes, Margaret. Yet that's an interesting way of looking at it."

"You know what I'm going to say, Rachel? If you want more, it's up to you. You're the one who thinks she has a lot to lose."

CHAPTER ELEVEN

Guests had been arriving all afternoon. Marie was away for the weekend, at Jack's insistence, enjoying her sixtieth birthday with Bill and her daughter's family. Jess had taken on the responsibility of ensuring the lodges, inside, were to the standard their visitors had come to expect, as well as her usual outside jobs. Jack hadn't stopped either, enjoying every minute of it and it was only now that he was beginning to tire.

The last few days since the diagnosis had been difficult for everyone. Marie initially was devastated, but had proved to be as supportive as ever and had gone away grudgingly for the weekend. Jess, on the other hand, had been quiet, not wanting to show too much emotion and how she was really feeling.

Jack's thoughts were interrupted by the last guest to arrive. The name in the diary had been aggravating him since this morning, and the person standing in front of him looked vaguely familiar. Rachel had followed the woman in and held back, perusing the leaflets of places to visit and the activities that were available in the area. After booking the person in, Jack was still none the wiser as to where he had met her before.

"You think I look familiar, don't you, Mr. Hamilton?" The woman smiled smugly.

"My apologies. Is it that obvious?"

"I came here one weekend. Oh, about fifteen, sixteen years ago. Jess invited me, and I stayed at the house."

Rachel's interest was suddenly piqued, and she watched a myriad of emotions cross Jack's face after what had been irritation, by the guest's initial arrogance. Now it was plain. He didn't like this woman at all and neither did she. Jack glanced toward Rachel, and she then thought she saw disappointment. *Or was it sadness?* She couldn't work it out as it all disappeared and he looked back to his guest. Embarrassed at being caught eavesdropping, Rachel quickly feigned great interest in the leaflet she'd just picked up, but not being able to help herself, continued to listen.

"Ah yes, I do remember now. It was a long time ago. May I ask why you are here again? I don't remember Jess mentioning anything."

"I've come to see if she has as good a memory as you."

"Well I'm afraid she's not here."

"She still works here, though, doesn't she? I enquired before I booked."

Rachel looked up at the woman as Jack simultaneously glanced her way again. She turned to place the leaflet back and rolled her eyes as she actually read it, *The Ten Best Rock Faces to Climb*.

"I'm sure you recall, she more than works here, she is a part owner of the estate." Jack proudly smiled.

"Yes, I'm sorry. If you wouldn't mind telling her that I'm here and if she wishes to speak to me, you know where I'm staying. I would appreciate that." The wretched smile appeared again. "I don't want it to be too much of a shock."

"I'll let Jess know. Is there anything else?"

"No, I think you have covered everything, thank you."

"Would you like to be shown to your lodge?"

"That's fine, I'd like to see if I can remember my way around."

"Very good."

Rachel noted the relief in Jack's voice and the fact he didn't push it. It would be usual for Jess to be summoned to escort a guest to their lodge and make sure they were happy with the facilities and how they worked. Not necessarily someone who had stayed before, but this woman hadn't, not in a lodge anyway.

***

Later that same day Rachel sat waiting on her balcony for Jess. She was bringing over a detailed map of the larch wood trail, a circular walk of around eight miles. Off the walk, there were apparently magnificent waterfalls and she desperately wanted to paint them. She hoped Jess would actually offer to take her.

She scolded herself again as her mind wandered to the strange woman. She was curious as to who she was. She had to be more to Jess than just a friend. She muttered, "Jess might tell you, give her a chance. Forget it, please." Spotting Jess walking up the path, she called, "Come straight up."

"Sorry I'm late." Jess plunked herself down in a chair. "Uncle Jack was tired and said he was going to go to bed early, so I waited until he went up. I think he overdid it today. Although I can't deny he's enjoyed it. It's good to see." She looked up at Rachel as she was handed a glass of wine. "Thanks. All the guests have booked in, and I have the emergency mobile with me, so I can relax."

"Good."

Jess watched as Rachel sat. "I have the route, but wondered if you would like some company? The map is pretty detailed, but it's not as easy to the falls as it looks."

Rachel's heart rate instantly increased. "I was planning on going tomorrow. But I could go on Monday instead?" Her voice sounded a little excited too.

Jess chuckled. "I've been given the day off tomorrow. In fact, I was almost ordered. Don and Jean will be around all day. I'm just to make sure I have this on me." She patted the mobile radio in her pocket.

"Sundays tend to be busy though, don't they? And Marie's away."

"Yes, I know. But I've been told in no uncertain terms that they can manage fine." Jess mimicked Jack's voice. "Anything the two old men can't deal with, we'll just leave for you later. Wouldn't want you to feel we can run the place without you."

Rachel laughed.

The evening rolled into the early hours before Jess found herself heading back down to the house. She had immediately relaxed when she'd spotted Rachel on the balcony, staring at the stars, not an obvious care in the world.

She, on the other hand, had been on edge and angry. When Uncle Jack had told her who was staying in Leven Lodge, she couldn't believe it. What on earth would possess Alison, after all these years, to appear? How could she even think Jess would want to see her, let alone speak to her? Her uncle's words echoed in her head. "If you wish to speak to her, you know where to find her."

She had no wish to speak to her.

CHAPTER TWELVE

Looking forward to the day ahead, Rachel rose early. Packing up the sandwiches she chuckled at the extra she'd made up for Jess. "What an appetite that woman has."

Last night had turned out to be so relaxing, she marveled at how close they had become over the past few months. It was as if she had known Jess for years. What had started as sexual inquisitiveness had developed into a firm friendship and now... She quickly reprimanded herself and then sighed. This time it wasn't an infatuation with someone she didn't know. She wanted Jess the person, as a friend and lover. Someone to share her life with.

She groaned and went back to her packing, only to be haunted by images of Jess looking at her. Dark, dilated pools of blue would undress her, piece of clothing by piece of clothing, until Rachel felt completely exposed and could almost feel Jess's touch. It never made her feel uncomfortable and she would never dream to mention it. Jess was either unaware she was doing it, or she just didn't realize it was plain to see on her face. The desire was palpable, yet Jess never yielded, never lost control. Rachel sighed.

***

She and Jess spent the morning slowly wandering up to the falls. It was a wonderful day, the sun shone brightly and a light breeze kept the day comfortable. Jess carried the food and water in a backpack and had a pair of binoculars hanging around her neck. She named the array of flowers they passed and any birds they saw, or even heard. She also started to name all the peaks along the mountain ridge, until she saw Rachel's face. She loved the look of them, but she would never remember all those names. She couldn't even pronounce most of them.

Rachel had carried her sketching and basic watercolor materials. There were so many opportunities to put pencil to paper and as they exited a forest, consisting mainly of alder and oak, Rachel was taken aback by the view. They overlooked a fast-flowing river that tumbled over rocks and around boulders, carving out the deepest gorge Rachel had ever seen. To her right were the waterfalls, three cascades, and they were as beautiful as Jess had described. She looked up, the river was obviously much wider at the top of the first fall, but that couldn't be seen, and as the water tumbled over the edge it was forced into a much narrower area. The pool at its base was dark and only appeared to sedately ripple, considering the battering it was receiving from above. A huge boulder sat at the pool's edge, blocking the water's continued flow to the river below, forcing it to go around and resulting in two lower falls. The speed of the water didn't slow, if anything it appeared to fall faster and the noise was deafening. She tapped Jess on the shoulder to attract her attention and shouted, "What are those amazing trees?" They were overhanging the gorge, clinging on desperately to the rock as they were showered in water.

"Birch. Incredible aren't they?" Jess smiled as she watched Rachel shake her head and look in awe.

***

After lunch Rachel returned to her sketching. Her ears had eventually stopped feeling like they were stuffed with cotton wool. The peace amongst the sparsely growing larch and juniper was the perfect contrast to the roar of the falls. Watching Jess, she produced a number of sketches she herself would treasure, especially one of Jess stretched out for a rest, a hat over her face. Her close-fitting vest outlined the curve of her breasts and the peak of her nipples, which slowly rose and fell as she dozed. Rachel's pencil continued downward to a stomach so firm and flat, then to a small amount of pale, soft skin exposed between vest and shorts. She scanned down the crossed, lean, muscular legs and then smiled at thick ankle socks and a large pair of walking boots. Jess gave off an air of someone who was comfortable with herself, totally unaware of how magnificent she looked to others. There was no arrogance in the way she held herself. Not like Michelle, she thought bitterly.

They climbed further up the hill, way off the beaten track, where Rachel saw all number of chicks in a variety of boxes and nests. When they reached the plateau of the hill, Jess took her to a gloriously hidden lochan where they spotted a female otter with her young, playing in the water. Heading down the other side into a forest of Scots pine, Jess pointed out evidence of pine martins and wildcat. The highlight, though, was the nest of a Scottish crossbill. It was deep in a thicket and they had to climb a nearby tree in order to see it through the binoculars. A brood of six, a record in Jess's book. The chicks were close to leaving the nest and filled it to overflowing, glimpses of wing and beak visible through the tangled bush. The parents were frantically rushing in and out feeding gaping and hungry mouths.

***

As the lodges came back into sight, Rachel realized how tired she was, yet extremely content with the entire day. The mysterious woman at the lodge had not entered her thoughts since this morning, and Jess hadn't mentioned her at all. Neither had she appeared preoccupied. Rachel thought it peculiar; the woman obviously wanted to see Jess. Maybe she had already seen her? But when? Jess had been with Jack and then her until almost one in the morning, and then they were up early and out for the day.

Jess was enjoying the quiet of the early evening as they strolled back toward home. Rachel had been like an excited kid all afternoon. She'd paid strict attention to any instructions, asked dozens of questions and soaked up every bit of information Jess provided. Jess looked over her shoulder to see Rachel with her head down. She stopped to ask her if she was all right. Rachel continued to walk, not noticing Jess had stopped in her path.

"Whoa," Jess cried, as she quickly placed her hands either side of Rachel's waist.

Rachel looked straight into those beautiful, blue, sparkling eyes, as hands burned an imprint on her waist. The eyes slowly started to dilate, boring deeply into hers. She was hypnotized by the sheer desire she saw. *Kiss me, Jess. Kiss me, please?*

Eventually realizing that wasn't going to happen, Rachel struggled to steady her breathing and huskily said without thinking, "The woman in Leven Lodge, who is she?"

Instantly she regretted her question. The face inches from her froze and the eyes contracted, blinking twice. Almost simultaneously the hands dropped from her waist.

Rachel gripped Jess's arm. "I'm sorry, I didn't mean to pry. I'm tired and my curiosity got the better of me."

Jess glanced at Rachel's hand before turning around and starting down the hill. "Come on, let's go."

Rachel quickly followed. It was evident Jess wasn't going to answer her question, and Rachel wanted to know why the woman had such an effect on her. "I take it you were not expecting her to visit?"

Jess sighed and stopped. "I haven't heard anything from her in sixteen years. Wouldn't a normal person write, or even telephone first? Surely they wouldn't just turn up, unless they meant trouble."

Rachel looked cautiously at Jess. "It depends if the person they wanted to see was likely to hide, or disappear."

Jess had to smile, but only slightly. "She did say to Uncle Jack that if I wished to speak to her, I knew where to find her. I actually have no desire to speak to her, so I don't think that's hiding."

"I suppose that's one way of looking at it."

Jess continued to walk and silence fell once again.

Probing further, Rachel quietly asked, "Did she hurt you?"

A variety of expressions passed over Jess's face, notably anguish. "Hurt me." She took a deep breath. "No, we hurt someone else."

Rachel suddenly sucked in a breath. "She had a partner and you had an affair with her, didn't you! Was her partner such a lousy lover she had you on the side to satisfy that need?"

Jess thought she was actually going to throw up. Reaching out, she took Rachel's hand. It was immediately pulled away, but Jess clung on. The hand didn't fight back, only stiffened. A few moments passed without any words and then Jess reached over with her other hand to smooth back a strand of hair that had fallen across a stern and flushed face. The hand in hers ever so slightly relaxed. She looked deep into dark eyes, before caressing and cupping a cheek. "I never meant to hurt Gretchen and—I certainly never meant to hurt you."

Rachel curled her thumb around the hand that held hers and lowered her gaze, leaning slightly into the hand touching her face. She sighed softly. "I think it's my turn to apologize. I'm not entirely sure where that came from." She tentatively looked up. "I really must be tired, I'm sorry."

Jess drew her hand down the cheek again. "There's no need to apologize, you've obviously been hurt and I reminded you of that."

Rachel swallowed hard. "You are nothing like Michelle, and I learned a long time ago you can't always blame the other woman. Easy though it is."

Jess looked unconvinced. "Nevertheless…"

"No Jess." Rachel clasped the hand that was in danger of moving away. "She had a number of affairs. I actually forgave her for one of them. The last one though…" She shook her head. "Well, we won't go into the details there." She sighed. "There were others I found out about after I had left her. Those I never forgave her for either."

Jess was completely at a loss for words. How could anyone possibly do that to this woman and, to make matters worse, let her catch them in the act? Rachel didn't need to voice that, it was obvious without the explanation. "I can't believe she would do that to you. With you as a partner she had to be extremely desperate for sex, or a self-obsessed fool. In fact, she must have been both."

Rachel was a little stung by the response. It was actually a compliment, a backhanded one, but a compliment all the same.

She squeezed the fingers twitching in hers. "Come on, we've gotten far too serious. I won't have Michelle spoiling our day. She most certainly isn't worth it."

Jess nodded. "And neither is Alison."

As they reached Lomond Lodge, Rachel stepped forward and pulled Jess into a hug. "Thank you, I have had a super day and I don't want to have spoiled it with my stupid musings."

The feel of Rachel's arms around her and the warm breath tickling her neck as she spoke, felt wonderful. Jess responded by wrapping her arms around Rachel's waist to pull her closer. She could feel her heart start to race, but before she could even contemplate what was going on or decide what she was going to do next, the mobile radio crackled into life. "Jess, come in Jess."

She grappled to release the thing from her hip. "Jess here."

As soon as she answered Rachel knew there was a problem. She riffled in her backpack for the Jeep's keys.

"We've just arrived at Rachel's lodge; we can be there in less than five," Jess said.

She ran around to the passenger side and hopped in, dropping her bag and binoculars at her feet.

Rachel asked as she started the engine, "What's going on?"

"An accident out on Forcan Ridge. A father and son have fallen. The mother's stayed with them, the older son came down to get help. Mark's on his way to pick me up."

"Why?"

"I'm a mountain rescue volunteer. Sorry, didn't you know? I usually do the winter months. I told them I'd help out if they were stretched." She shrugged. "They must be stretched."

As they turned into the yard, Mark's Land Rover appeared and so did a welcoming party. Jess immediately got out, popped her head back in the door and beamed at Rachel. "Thanks for a great day. I didn't mean to spoil it either. Quits I hope?" Don, Jean and Jack threw equipment into the back of Mark's vehicle, Jess jumped in and they were gone.

***

It was three thirty when Jess arrived home exhausted. The rescue had been a tricky one. The father had sustained a complicated fracture to the thigh, lost a good deal of blood and was in a state of shock. The boy had an obvious concussion and the difficulty lay in his assessment. Whether his hysteria was due to a possible brain injury, or the situation and tiredness it was initially difficult to tell. Jess believed it was the latter as time passed and the boy became increasingly clingy. She'd ended up having to go to the hospital when he wouldn't let go. Eventually she left a grateful mother and son, with a father in surgery and a sleeping younger sibling.

Sitting on the edge of her bed, in the dark, she stripped, leaving her clothes in a heap on the floor. Lying down, she looked up to see the moon lighting a painting Rachel had given her. Jess fell asleep thinking it was beyond her comprehension how Michelle could have affairs when she had Rachel waiting at home.

CHAPTER THIRTEEN

Jess groaned and flopped back onto her pillow. It was only seven and she wanted more sleep, yet her mind wouldn't let her. She was due to take her uncle Jack to see the consultant again this morning, to discuss his prognosis and what options were available in palliative treatments and care. She sighed.

She lay there as thoughts tumbled around in her head. She hadn't really talked to her uncle about what she saw as his death sentence. Then there was Rachel. Images of yesterday when she could quite easily have taken Rachel where she stood. It would relieve the building pressure cooker inside her, if she could just have sex with her and be done with it. Her problem, though, was that she wanted more than just sex with Rachel, but couldn't really work out what. The thought scared her. One thing she was sure of: she couldn't fall in love with her. That would be a disaster. Panic started to set in and she sat up quickly. *She is just so goddamn beautiful, that's all it is. Get a grip.* She thought of the times they'd spent together. *No one is that easy to be with. The way she moves, the way she laughs, the way she does everything!* It could only end in Rachel being hurt and the last person she wanted to harm was Rachel. The woman had already been badly treated by someone who'd supposedly loved her, reducing her sexual self-esteem to virtually zero. She needed a person who could commit wholly and take the time in coaxing her to enjoy the physical side of a relationship. Not someone who could only offer a quick roll in the hay. Jess smiled. Well, she could extend it to a few rolls in the hay. She sighed, defeated. Rachel deserved better than that, a better person than her.

Another problem suddenly threw itself into the cauldron of her mind. Alison. Why was she here? Well, if she went and spoke to her she would find out. Sex, that's all they had. Could she relieve some sexual frustration? *What on earth are you thinking? She doesn't deserve the time of day. Not yours anyway.*

She rubbed her face. She was tired, that's all it was. Out on the landing her uncle passed her door and headed down the stairs. Silent tears instantly began to run down her face.

It was a few minutes before she wiped her eyes and picked up the telephone. "Hi Julie, it's Jess. I'm sorry to ring so early, I need to see you—yes, tomorrow night will be fine."

***

The day proved to be long and Jess was exhausted from the lack of sleep. The consultant had been positive in his options for Uncle Jack's palliative treatment. Yet she couldn't get past the three to four months prognosis. He had again refused any invasive treatment and in her heart she understood why. It would only prolong the inevitable and not necessarily improve the quality of the time he had left. Pain relief had been covered in greater depth—this was going to be his major problem. She paid particular attention to this part to ensure Tom was fully informed of what lay ahead and may be required. She and Marie could hopefully manage with any care until the latter stages, when a nurse would be employed. It was her uncle's wish to stay at home, unless it proved impossible or too difficult for those around him.

After the consultant they had visited the mountain-rescued family, finding them all looking a hundred percent better. Even the father after surgery, leg pinned and immobilized, looked the picture of health. A far cry from how Jess felt, but it cheered her to see them.

The afternoon she'd spent with Mark and Lewis, one of the volunteer coordinators, writing up a report of the night's events and why Jess had been involved. She ended the session grateful for being purely a winter volunteer, where the job and not the politics were more important.

Quietly entering the house, she stepped into the kitchen and glanced at the clock: nine thirty. Completely drained of any physical or emotional energy she leaned against the door frame. Marie was busy at the stove and hadn't heard her come in. "That smells good."

Marie turned around. She gave a sad smile and pulled out a chair at the table. "Hi, come and take a seat. It's a chicken casserole and you can be my taster."

Jess attempted a smile and slumped down in the offered chair. "Uncle Jack gone up to bed?"

"Yes, he was a little tired."

Jess let out a heavy sigh. "Oh Marie, I'm so selfish. I don't want Uncle Jack to die, and I don't know what to do about it."

Marie placed a reassuring hand on her shoulder. "I know. This isn't easy for anyone. Things will get better though."

Jess turned quickly in her chair and looked at Marie with disbelieving eyes. "Better, how on earth can it get better?"

Marie sat down and took her hand. "I've been through all that Jess, and we have to be strong for your uncle."

"I'm trying."

She sighed. "Oh Jess, he knows you're suffering. He wants to leave everything in order, but above all else, he wants to leave knowing we will all be happy. He can't know that without speaking about it."

"But…Happy, how the hell can I be happy?"

"Not in the short term, in the long term. You have a life ahead of you. He just wants to know you will be all right." Tears began to well in Marie's eyes. "He doesn't want to think of you spending the rest of your life alone."

Confused and irritated that everyone appeared to be worrying about her being alone, she snapped at Marie. "That's not what's bothering me. You will still be here, and I have friends. I won't be alone. Why does everyone think that?" She sighed, knowing she was being childish. "I won't have him. That's what's bothering me."

The reception area bell interrupted them.

Marie quickly rose to her feet. "I'll go."

Jess caught Marie's hand. "No, I'm sorry. I'll go."

Marie gave her a quick hug. "We'll talk when you get back."

Jess looked at the pan on the stove. "Could I please have plate of that too and some crusty bread as well?"

Jess walked into the reception area and frowned at the person standing in front of her. "Bloody hell, it's you, isn't it?"

"Well, that's a welcome if ever I heard one."

Jess quickly tried to rein in her temper and the urge to throw her out. "Alison." Taking a very deep breath she positioned herself behind the desk. "Did you want something? It's late and I'm tired."

Alison smirked then replied, "I hope you don't greet all your guests in this manner? I was about to say, you haven't changed a bit, you still look absolutely fantastic."

Jess looked Alison up and down. *Well you have and not for the better I might add.* The thought relaxed her a little. "Thank you, but what can I do for you?"

"I was hoping we could talk?"

Jess raised an eyebrow. "I thought you told my uncle if I wished to talk to you, I would know where to find you?"

Alison stepped forward. "I hoped you'd have been, at least, a little curious. I wasn't expecting to have to wait for two days, with nothing to do and then come and find you."

Nothing to do! Jess couldn't believe it. Her uncle had remembered that she had invited herself the last time as well, and that Jess had spent the time attempting to entertain a person who had no interest in the outdoors, at all. She obviously still didn't. So why was she here? Jess folded her arms across her chest. "Alison, you still haven't answered my question, what do you want?"

Alison placed a hand on the desk separating them. "I came to see you. To talk to you."

Jess was losing patience. This day couldn't get much worse. "Talk away."

"Can we go somewhere a little more comfortable?"

"No Alison. This has been a long day and my dinner is waiting for me."

Alison moved around to the side of the desk, and Jess felt suddenly claustrophobic. Alison was bigger than she remembered. "Listen Jess, I know it's been a long time. You may not believe this, but a day has not gone by where I haven't thought of you. It's true. What we had back then was something special, and I've regretted letting you go ever since."

Jess couldn't comprehend what she was hearing. "You never let me go. I left."

Alison closed the gap further. "I gave you no choice."

Jess snorted. "Please don't tell me you've come back to rekindle what we had sixteen years ago."

"I hoped we might at least get to know each other again and see if the flame still burned. I know mine for you hasn't been extinguished."

Jess grinned incredulously. "You were always good with the sweet talk, that hasn't changed."

Alison touched Jess's arm. "Does that mean we still have a flicker?"

Jess shrugged her arm out of Alison's reach. "No, it doesn't. Don't be so ridiculous. There will never be anything between us again, so don't even fool yourself."

Alison frowned. "Do you have someone else?"

"That, Alison, is none of your business." Jess was beginning to feel uncomfortable. Was this woman serious?

Alison looked at her confidently. "I don't think you have. You wouldn't still be living with your uncle."

"This is where I live and work. Why wouldn't I still be living here?"

Alison ignored her question. "I know I hurt you, and I want to let you know how sorry I am."

Jess was dumbstruck at the audacity of the woman to think she had that great an influence over her life. She went to say something but fell silent. *Damn.* The woman was right. She had been a warning that getting involved with someone had a cost and that cost was too great. "Alison, I really am hungry and tired. Can we talk about this tomorrow?" Jess could hear the weakness in her voice. She couldn't fight it tonight and she knew this woman wasn't going to go easily.

Alison smiled. A smug one Jess thought. "Fine with me. Until the morning then?"

Jess rolled her eyes. "Tomorrow, fine."

Alison stepped back. "Don't hide this time. I will still find you."

***

Rachel sighed with contentment as she slipped into bed. The lack of sleep the night before worrying about Jess and the frustrating day she'd had left her weary. She'd been attempting a set of illustrations for a new comic and they looked as lifeless as the day outside. Only the midges appeared to enjoy the damp, still days like today. Even the mountains that could usually relax her appeared weighed down with the mist that hung heavy over them. Scott, her agent, had also telephoned with the details of two more exhibitions and appearances she needed to make before returning home for her sister's wedding. And the arrangements had been finally confirmed for the launch of Michelle's book, which meant she would have to be in London at the beginning of November. She'd hoped to avoid the party, signings and publicity that would surround the release, but it seemed she had to be seen in public with the woman. There was some good news though, she could probably return here and travel to London as needed. That way she could spend as much time as possible with Jack. After her visit with him this afternoon, it seemed all the more important. She smiled. And, of course, she would see Jess.

CHAPTER FOURTEEN

More and more aroused, Jess opened her eyes to find Alison looking up at her from between her legs. Smiling triumphantly she exclaimed, "I'm going to make you come." Her head slowly lowered and Jess felt a tongue gently stroke at her swollen folds. She tried to move, yet couldn't. The pressure was building and all she could do was clutch the sheets. She hadn't wanted this woman touching her again, let alone giving her this much pleasure. She couldn't understand what had happened and fighting the feeling now was futile. Suddenly a rush of blood pounded all her senses and washed through her body and she shuddered as she climaxed. She started to weep; she had not wanted to give in to Alison. A voice cooed in her ear, reassuring her everything would be all right as she was pulled in to a tight hug and fingers ran through her hair. She began to relax and opened her eyes to find Rachel smiling that adorable smile of hers and then devilishly licking her lips before leaning into her and capturing the ones she had her eyes on.

Jess blurted something, not understanding quite what, and scrambled to sit up. Her body glistened with sweat as she looked around the room. "Good grief! It's a dream." She slumped back onto her pillow, gasping, "What a nightmare."

Getting back to sleep after that was impossible. The thought of another dream...Although the thought of Rachel playing both roles, wasn't in the least unpleasant, in fact it was just a little too pleasing. *I'm going mad.* She rolled out of bed and threw herself under the shower.

Heading out with a cup of tea to the wooded glade, to watch the birds fight over food at the feeders, she reviewed her conversation with Alison. She was disappointed in her reaction. "Why was I so weak?" If she was going to have to speak to Alison she wanted to be firm. Basically tell the woman where to go. She shook her head, exasperated at the thought that Alison wanted to rekindle something they'd had donkey's years ago.

The only good thing she could muster out of seeing Alison was the reassurance that time had definitely quenched her lust for the woman. There was no chance of a sexual encounter despite her dream. She frowned and bit her bottom lip. The same couldn't be said for Alison. "Jess Brewster, you're not weak," she told herself.

***

Rachel could hear what she thought were heated voices as she approached the barn at the back of the house.

"Alison, I thought I made it clear last night."

"You said some things and then proclaimed you were tired. You didn't want to hear what I had to say, that's why you agreed to talk to me today."

"Alison, you turn up after sixteen years, late at night expecting me to talk, so I talked. What more do you want?"

"You," came the short seductive remark.

Rachel had reached the barn door but stood to the side out of sight. She couldn't help but listen.

Alison stepped toward Jess. "Look, Jess, I made a huge mistake back then. I loved you and I couldn't help myself. You were fun and so—"

"Gullible!" Jess interrupted.

Alison smiled. "Innocent. You were a delight. I enjoyed life when I was with you. I still feel the same as I did then. I've never forgotten what we had, how you made me feel."

There was silence and Rachel felt ill. They must be kissing. She wasn't sure what to do. If she moved they might hear her. Yet the last thing she wanted to hear was Jess making love to someone other than her.

Then Alison continued. "You know I love you Jess and you did say that you would always love me, I remember those words."

"Love! What a heap of nonsense. That so-called love nearly cost someone her life. Have you forgotten the pain you caused Gretchen? I caused Gretchen." Her face reddened with anger and she could hear her voice rise with every word. "She cried on my shoulder for weeks, yes weeks, don't you remember? Telling me all about her unfaithful lover and cursing the bitch who was stealing her away. If I had known that bitch was me, I..." She let out a heavy breath. "For goodness sake, Alison, she tried to kill herself!"

"What would you have done? What Jess? Could you in all honesty say you would have stopped seeing me if you had known?"

Jess closed her eyes, shaking her head as if to clear it. All she could feel was an erupting headache. "Yes, I would have. Now, please, just go."

As she attempted to pass, Alison gripped her arm. "I'm not sure I believe that."

Jess shook her head. "Believe what you like."

The grip tightened. "Jess, I'm sorry, I know I handled the whole affair all wrong, but you swept me off my feet." She looked searchingly into Jess's eyes. "I never thought I'd upset you that much, you just walked away."

"You never upset me, not in the way you think, and, for the record, I never swept you off your feet, you came running after me. I didn't know what hit me."

"I didn't hear you complaining." She smiled, speaking softly, "You were irresistible, and I wanted a chance with you. See where things would go. Once I'd lied about not having a girlfriend, I didn't seem to be able to tell you the truth. I felt guilty the entire time." She waited. Jess didn't reply. "I explained that to you, and all you did was give me an ultimatum. You or Gretchen? I couldn't leave Gretchen, not after what she'd done."

Exasperated, Jess took a deep breath. "Alison, that's why I gave you the ultimatum, I knew you wouldn't leave her. You were a coward from the outset or you would have told me about her in the first place. I didn't want to leave any doubt that I wouldn't be coming back."

Alison's grip grew firmer still. "But I loved you."

Jess shrugged her arm. "You're hurting me." Alison instantly let go. "That didn't matter then and it doesn't matter now. I *found* her, Alison. I thought she was dead. I was so happy when they revived her. And then *you* entered that hospital room. I felt physically sick and disgusted, I couldn't believe my eyes. *You* were her lover, and I was the one who drove Gretchen to take her own life." The feelings of disgust hit her again. "You're not the only coward. I walked away and left Gretchen to you."

Alison reached for her hand. "I'm sorry. You will never know how sorry I am. Believe me when I say, I never cheated again. I learned my lesson."

Jess pulled away. "I'm afraid I find that hard to believe." She sighed. "I can't judge you. I don't know you and I never really did."

As she started to move away, Alison desperately clutched at her arm again. "Please, Jess. If it helps? I got my comeuppance, Gretchen did the same to me and only after I had wasted a further fourteen years of my life."

Rachel's sadness at what she had heard and her guilt at eavesdropping on a very private conversation were suddenly extinguished by a flare of temper. Michelle had said those exact same words when Rachel told her to leave, and she wasn't even the one having the affair. Taking a deep breath, she steadied herself and breezed into the barn to stop the distress this woman was obviously dredging up in Jess. "Oh sorry, I thought I heard voices. Morning, Jess, is my bike ready?"

Rachel looked straight at Jess. The strain in her face was apparent. Rachel wanted nothing more than to run over, take her into her arms and soothe that look away. Instead, she produced what she thought was her most perfect smile. Relief flooded Jess's face, followed by a blush.

Jess yanked her arm from Alison's grasp and started toward Rachel. "Morning, Rachel, I have your bicycle over here. It's all ready for you." She looked over her shoulder. "Excuse me, Ms. Carpenter."

Rachel stepped forward and whispered, "Is there anything I can do?"

Jess couldn't help herself; she was lost in those rich brown eyes. "You could kiss me. That might make her go away." Not believing what had stumbled out of her mouth, she blurted, "Sorry I...I..."

Rachel felt a glow grow all over her. She had never seen anyone look so mortified and embarrassed by what they had said. Jess was the deepest shade of red from her chest to the tips of her ears. She continued to apologize and then talked at hundred miles an hour as she tightened up the saddle and went over how to use the gears.

Rachel grinned. She had to save her. "It's okay; I know how it all works. I've ridden enough bikes in my time. I do need a helmet though." Jess handed the helmet over and Rachel could sense her relief. She smiled. "Thank you."

As Rachel pushed the bike out of the barn, she saw Alison standing to the side, obviously waiting for her to leave, so she could pounce on Jess, yet again. Rachel gave a heavy sigh, unsure as to whether she was disappointed at not being the one to take up Jess's morning or sorry for Jess, with what might be lying ahead.

As Rachel disappeared up the track, Jess gave a wave and called, "Take care." Footfalls were behind her. She turned to see Alison. Groaning, she asked, "What do you want now?"

CHAPTER FIFTEEN

Julie swung open the door. "Hi, come in. Sorry, I've got to rush back to the kitchen."

Jess grinned. "I'll see you in there." She closed the front door and placed her overnight bag at the bottom of the stairs.

Julie smiled as Jess walked into the kitchen. "So what's going on in that head of yours, besides Jack, Marie, Don and the lodges?"

Jess knew her friend was trying to make light of what probably sounded cryptic and not a little hysterical on the phone. She swallowed hard. "Rachel and Alison."

Julie frowned. "Alison? Who's Alison? Oh, my God. Not that Alison?"

Julie's reaction eased Jess's tension a little. "Yeah. That Alison. I'm surprised you remember her."

"How the hell could I forget her? She ruined your life!"

Jess chortled, relaxing. "I think that's a little extreme."

Julie grumped. "I don't think so. That woman single-handedly put you off relationships for life."

Jess sighed. She knew what Julie's reaction would be, so why was she surprised. And why did she really want to talk about this anyway? She replied. "No she didn't."

"Yes she bloody well did!" Julie stopped. "I'm not helping am I? Sorry."

"No. Maybe when we've eaten, I could cope with your advice for my array of problems. In fact, I'll look forward to it."

Julie nudged her with a shoulder. "You sure about that?"

Giving a sideways glance Jess conceded, "Not entirely."

***

Over dinner they talked about Jack, his illness and reminisced about past events. Mainly Jack's "lady friends" as they used to call them. "Do you remember Mrs. Jenkins? The one that rented the Douglas cottage."

Jess grimaced. "Why did you have to remind me about her? She scared the life out of me."

They had been thirteen and playing at being spies. Mrs. Jenkins was their target for the morning. It was noon and they had only listed one activity in their log in the last half hour. She'd become a boring subject since arriving at her home. Suddenly, Jack appeared from the other side of the house and tapped on the door. He was greeted with a kiss that seemed to go on forever, before Mrs. Jenkins pulled him inside. They'd looked at each other questioningly, and then sneaked down the hill to see what was going on.

Now Julie started to giggle as she stood and collected their plates. "It was your face when I told you what they were up to."

"Oh don't. I've never heard anything like it."

"Not heard a woman shouting yes, oh yes or grunting, snorting and screaming during sex? I don't believe it."

"Behave yourself. I have never experienced anything like that."

Julie continued to tease. "Come on, you know you have. Spill."

Jess shot back at her. "Have you grunted and snorted?"

Her friend gave a look of mock horror. "Me?"

She grinned. "Yes you, you're a woman, I could imagine you grunting like that."

Julie threw a napkin at her. "That's slanderous, how could you?"

"I bet you've done the yes, oh yes bit though." She lifted her eyebrows suggestively. "And the scream."

It was Julie's turn to blush as she replied, "Not quite in the same way."

Jess laughed, and then nodded, feigning seriousness. "I can relate to that. I hear that every time."

Julie slapped her playfully on the shoulder. "I bet."

***

They adjourned to the lounge with the wine and made themselves more comfortable. Jess felt wonderfully relaxed until she saw Julie's mouth open and close and a frown form across her brow. Julie would know she wouldn't bring up the subject of Rachel and Alison again, so she was obviously trying to formulate her introduction to the subject. She waited, prepared.

"How did Alison contact you? Did she write or phone?"

Jess sighed. "I should be so lucky, she just turned up."

"Turned up? You mean at the lodges?"

"Yes, and guess what? She wants to rekindle our relationship. Can you believe that?"

"I hope you told her where she could go rekindle herself?"

Jess grinned. "I did, but she doesn't seem to grasp the fact I have no interest in her anymore."

"Jess, you just need to tell her. For heaven's sake, it's been years."

"I did."

"Do you still fancy her or something, is that the problem?"

Jess spluttered, glaring at Julie. "Of course not. I must have been blind back then. For the life of me I can't see what I ever saw in her."

"It was the sex. You were like a kid in a sweetie shop for the very first time. You don't always care who's doing the dishing out."

Jess smirked. "Well whatever it was, it's not there anymore. I just wish she would go away and leave me alone. I just don't understand how someone could appear after sixteen years and declare their love. It's ridiculous."

"Does she still have a partner?"

"Actually, she did say Gretchen left her about a year ago." She shook head. "Amazing it was just a year ago." *I wonder if she ever knew.*

"That would give her enough time to work through her old girlfriends, I suppose. She'll be seeing if any of them are willing and available."

"You don't really think that's why she's here, do you?"

Julie laughed. "Oh I don't know, Jess, but it's as good a reason as any. You just need to be assertive. I could come up and get rid of her for you, if you like?"

"I think I can manage, she's only booked in for a week. If anyone's going to throttle her it'll be me." She paused. "It's just frustrating. If I had to deal with her and nothing else, it wouldn't be a problem. I just don't seem to be handling anything well at the moment."

Julie smiled softly. "It's understandable." They sat quietly for a while before Julie wandered over to refill Jess's empty wineglass. She quietly asked, "How is Rachel?"

"Fine."

Julie rolled her eyes. "You hinted at a problem earlier."

Jess shrugged. "Are you sure you can cope with more? I've done nothing but moan this evening."

"You haven't. You very rarely grumble about anything, give yourself a break." Chuckling she added, "You've had to listen to all my problems over the years."

"I don't know where to start, or how to explain. Maybe it'll sort itself out."

Julie ignored that. "I'm assuming we're still talking about Rachel."

"Yes."

"Are you struggling with just being friends?"

"I suppose. She's grown on me." She frowned at her friend. "She's charming, intelligent and very easy to be with. Actually she's rather…wonderful." She paused. "I'm becoming increasingly obsessed with her, or something like it. It really isn't good."

Julie leaned forward. "Why don't you think it's good?"

"She's been hurt badly before and by someone who supposedly loved her." She sighed. "And she let something slip inadvertently, which explains why she appeared happy with our friendship arrangement."

"What do you mean? Is she a practicing celibate?"

Jess chuckled. "Maybe she is." She shook her head. "No, I don't think so."

Julie's tone softened. "So, what is it? Would you like to make love to her?" Jess blushed and before she could respond, Julie continued. "That's what people in love want to do. I couldn't wait for Tom to kiss me and then more."

Jess frowned. "No."

"There's nothing wrong with wanting someone for more than sex. Rachel is a lovely woman. You could fall for a lot worse."

Jess paled. "No, it's not right. I'm not in love with her. Why would you say that?" She looked at Julie with pleading eyes. "No, no, you're wrong. I can't be. You know I can't be." She wiped her clammy hands on her trousers as she attempted to slow her racing heart.

Julie placed a hand on her restless friend. "It's obvious isn't it?"

"No!" The pounding in Jess's chest and head became unbearable. If she didn't calm them, she would pass out. She put her head in her hands, closed her eyes and concentrated on her breathing.

"Jess, are you all right?"

"Yes. Just give me a minute." A few moments passed before she turned to her worried friend. "I'm sorry. I don't know what came over me. I'm okay now, just a bit of a headache."

Julie spoke cautiously. "Are you panicking over possible feelings for Rachel?"

"Please, Julie, can we leave it?"

"I've never known anyone to affect you as she has. It's just different from anything you've experienced before. That's all. It's okay."

Jess tried to think, she couldn't shake the feeling of terror that lingered. Her head was still aching. "I don't know."

"I think it is." Julie frowned and took Jess's hand again.

Jess stammered. "With Alison the whole thing was new. We had to keep it quiet. Lecturer and student relationships were frowned upon." She looked at her friend. "Her story was plausible. What an idiot." She began to relax a little. "Kirsty. I loved her very much, but we were young."

Julie nodded and smiled softly. "I know." She squeezed Jess's hand. "Did either of them make you feel like this though?"

Jess leaned back. "Kirsty loved me too. But even she didn't know what it was all about." She sighed. "Then look what happened." She looked at her friend. "I don't ever remember feeling this out of control or confused though."

"Well then, you can't let this go by, Jess."

Jess stiffened, her heart picked up its pace again, along with the throbbing in her head. She glared at Julie. "I can and I will. Love is lethal—I will not go there. I only have to get through this next month and she'll be gone for the winter. Then I'll get over this stupid infatuation." The tone left no room for argument. The risk was too great. Jess believed her love was responsible for her family's death, Kirsty's death and Gretchen's attempted suicide.

***

Jess stood to give Julie a hand as she returned with cheese and biscuits. With Julie out of the room, it gave her the chance to regain her composure and give herself a good talking to. Putting the feelings she had for Rachel into perspective. She liked her, that's all it was. Everyone liked Rachel. Jess was struggling to cope with her uncle's illness and the successful spell the lodges were having. It was just causing her to blow things out of all proportion. It hadn't helped Alison appearing, bringing up painful memories, but she would be leaving soon. Good riddance to that one, Jess thought. Rachel though, she didn't want to leave. She sighed.

Julie looked at her friend. "I think I've figured out a way that could make it easier for you to put these feelings aside. It may sound a little harsh."

"Go on," Jess said reluctantly as she placed the food on the table. Julie opened another bottle of wine, deliberately avoiding eye contact. Jess waited and heard her friend take a deep breath.

"You have to stop thinking of yourself. If you can't give Rachel what you think she wants, or needs. You will just cause too much upset. You have to think of Rachel and Jack."

Jess stopped and stared at Julie, who still wouldn't look her way. *Selfish*. She couldn't believe it. Tears welled in her eyes. "You're right. I'm so wrapped up in how I feel. Uncle Jack is extremely fond of Rachel and if I hurt her—or even myself—he would be devastated. He doesn't have forever and his well-being and happiness are the most important things. They are the last people in the world I want to upset." Jess didn't want to think of life without Uncle Jack, but there was no getting past the fact, the doctor had only given him around three to four months. He was going to be her focus from now on. Jess was going to make the last few months anything Uncle Jack wanted them to be.

"Thank you."

Julie looked at her, tears trickling down her face. Jess smiled and opened her arms. "Come here. I know you're only trying to help me, and you have." Julie didn't say another word as they wrapped their arms tightly around one another.

***

The next couple of days were positive and eventful for Jess. Her uncle had accompanied her while she worked around the estate, tiring by midafternoon, so it was perfect timing for his teas with Rachel. She'd discussed with Tom the options for her uncle's pain relief and the help he would offer. Basically he would be available twenty-four hours a day, for whatever reason. Tom also told her he would look into nursing options for further down the line and made it quite clear to Jess not to allow Jack to put off asking for help, or mentioning the slightest of problems. Changes at this stage could be rapid and it was best not to delay. Her mood was low after the visit, yet it was all important information and she absorbed every single word.

She'd spent a short time with Alison and had decided they had absolutely nothing in common and had said as much to her. Alison had then made it quite clear she wouldn't give up. Jess had fleetingly considered succumbing in an attempt to quash her sexual frustration. But the need wasn't there with Alison; it only reared its ugly head when Rachel was within her sights. Alison should have been gone by now, but she'd found out the family following her into the lodge had been delayed by a couple of days, so she had decided to stay. Why, Jess couldn't comprehend, and she didn't particularly care anymore.

CHAPTER SIXTEEN

Rachel walked out onto the porch and breathed the air in deeply, attempting to dispel the annoyance left after her telephone conversation with Scott. He had called with further details about the signing and release of Michelle's book. He was livid at the fact that it was all about the writer and very little about the artist. Rachel had warned him what it would be like collaborating on another book. So here she was, being dictated to by Michelle, yet again. He argued that it would not be like that. "Over my dead body," he'd said. If only Rachel would trust him and give him full rein over what she did regarding the launch. So she had, giving him full responsibility, consoling herself in the fact that he had never let her down and had only been good for her. Nevertheless, it made her uncomfortable.

She took another deep breath and started walking down the track. "Don't let it get to you. It is a wonderful day. You are in a place that you adore and are surrounded by breathtaking scenery and..." She stopped, and stared down into the yard of the house. "People."

Jess was basked in sunshine. Her tanned, toned body was covered in sparkling perspiration, emphasizing every contour as it glided with each move she made. Rachel's heart beat faster as she consciously told herself to breathe.

After a moment she caught sight of something in the trees opposite. Alison was hiding, or at least watching. "That's sick," she gasped, imagining the thrill Alison was experiencing. *Great, who am I to talk.*

Rachel felt an urgency to stop all the voyeurism and strode briskly down toward the woman who was providing everyone's entertainment. Wood was everywhere in orderly piles, from kindling to huge trunks. After Jess took a swing, she called, "Morning, you look busy."

Jess turned and beamed such a radiant smile that the warmth of it caused Rachel's body temperature to instantly rise. Breathlessly, Rachel continued. "Don't look around, but you have an audience not far from here. Alison."

Jess was only fleetingly tempted to look. Rachel was much more interesting in her light-colored shorts and dark green vest. They showed off her stunningly bronzed and curved body, shining hair and big brown eyes. All Jess wanted to do at that moment was wrap her dirty, sweaty body around this woman and ravish her. Swallowing hard and blinking her eyes a couple of times, she made a vain attempt to muster a coherent word. "Hi." She'd completely forgotten why she wasn't to look anywhere, other than into those eyes.

Rachel stopped and when her eyes fixed on the ones staring right back at her, they instantly began to darken and glaze over. The desire yet again was transparent. She moved forward until she was within inches of Jess and lowered her gaze to full red lips that were slightly parted. She desperately wanted to touch them with her own. She heard herself croak as she closed the distance between them further. "Jess, I'm going to kiss you." Cupping her hand gently around Jess's head, she guided her down to meet her waiting lips. She pressed softly, then teased and stroked the mouth she had claimed, tentatively sliding the tip of her tongue inside.

Jess moaned. Her head was spinning and her legs were in danger of buckling. She placed her hands on Rachel's hips to try and steady herself, but she wanted more. Rachel's breasts were pushing against her as hands slid over her shoulders. Her arms went around Rachel's waist pulling her closer. She felt nipples harden. She moved a hand down to Rachel's buttocks and pulled her tight to her center that was throbbing with uncontrollable need. She would have taken Rachel there and then, if it was not for her head betraying her. She dragged her lips away from the ones providing the intoxicating pleasure and tried to focus her gaze on Rachel's and was met with pure need and wanting. Pushing Rachel away she grasped both shoulders and held her at arm's length, heaving ragged breaths. "I can't do this Rachel, I'm sorry, I just can't."

Rachel tried to move forward, but Jess was too strong. "Why not? Please."

The pleading eyes almost undid what little resolve Jess had mustered. "I'll only hurt you and I don't want to do that. Please just believe me that I can't." Jess swallowed hard as her senses returned.

"Well isn't this just dandy," a voice said behind her. She looked at Rachel who was also attempting to compose herself.

Jess shook her head and clutched at her chest that was pounding way too fast, and then turned to Alison. "What did you say?"

"Maybe I was wrong about you not having someone else. But it seems to me it's not what you want," Alison said triumphantly before looking straight at Rachel. "She never pushed me away. You obviously don't have what it takes." A wicked smile crossed her face.

Rachel was too stunned to respond.

Jess took two steps toward Alison, grabbed her by the arm and started pushing her up the path. "Right, that's it." Rage was flooding her senses. "Rachel has more to offer than you ever did. She has more decency flowing through her veins than both of us put together. Now, I want you out of that lodge and off these premises before the end of the day."

Alison turned around and confidently said, "There's no need to get upset. I'm going today anyway." She looked back at Rachel and said to Jess, "I know why you pushed her away. No one throws away the chance if a beautiful woman thrusts themselves upon them, unless they have feelings for someone else." A smug, seedy grin lifted her lips.

"For heaven's sake, Alison, what is the matter with you? I don't find you the least bit attractive, or appealing. In fact, I'm finding it hard to fathom what I saw in you in the first place." She threw her hands up with exasperation. "Why don't you just go and visit a gay bar? You'll find plenty of willing women there."

Alison looked shocked at the idea. "I don't need to pick women up in bars." She looked at Rachel then back at Jess. "Is that what you've been doing all these years?"

Jess glared at her. "It beats screwing up other people's lives. Maybe you should try it." They looked coldly at each other for a moment before Jess sighed. "Oh, goodbye Alison, I hope you find what you're looking for."

Alison gave a defeated smile and dropped her head slightly. "Goodbye Jess, I won't bother you again." She turned and headed slowly up the hill.

Half smiling, Rachel raised her eyebrows and said, "Well you were right. You said a kiss would make her go away."

Jess slowly grinned. "I did, didn't I?"

They both began to laugh.

CHAPTER SEVENTEEN

Jess quietly lounged on the oversized and overstuffed sofa in the middle of the observation room. She watched through the picture window as two young fox cubs tumbled over one another. Their mother was cautiously stretched out close by, keeping her eye on them.

The last week had gone in a flash. There had been no time to dwell on the feeling of unbridled pleasure she'd experienced from the kiss. Nor the drama that had gone with it that morning.

Uncle Jack had been through a difficult period after, according to Tom, probably trying to do too much around the estate. Although her uncle wasn't having any of that. Emergency jobs appeared on a daily basis, and she had seriously considered employing some help. As soon as she did, she knew the work would tail off and her uncle wouldn't like her hanging about the house, watching his every move.

She hadn't seen Rachel for a couple of days. This was her second trip away, attending an exhibition. It actually suited her fine that Rachel was staying out of her way and that she would be gone soon, returning to the States in just under two weeks. The only problem was that she missed her company.

Looking over at the door Jess jumped out of her seat. "Rachel!"

She smiled. "Sorry, I didn't mean to startle you."

"What are you doing here?" As her heart raced she tried to give off an air of calm. "I didn't realize you were back."

Rachel wandered over to the window. "I scared your cubs. I don't suppose they'll be back?"

Jess stood by her side. "Afraid not and I think it was me that actually frightened them off." Her heart was not slowing and the smell of Rachel's shampoo was doing nothing to help. She turned to look at her as Rachel said, "Marie asked me to come and get you. They're having tea in the conservatory."

Rachel relaxed once they were sat down and engaged in conversation with Marie and Jack. Her feelings of wanting rushed back when she saw Jess relaxed on the sofa. They had laughed the kiss off but the few times they'd spoken since, the tension was undeniable. Rachel had been grateful to be able to avoid Jess. She was struggling with both her feelings and Jess's mixed ones.

"I believe you haven't been well Jack?" Rachel watched as Marie and Jess exchanged a smile and realized why when Jack answered.

"Who told you that?"

"Julie. I picked up a few things on my way up."

"I'm fine. A lot of fuss about nothing. I'll have to have words with that Tom."

"Oh, don't be silly you old fool, you can't stop people worrying."

Jess grinned in Rachel's direction at Marie's words and then added, "Tom said he overdid it."

Jack snapped. "Don't you start."

Jess laughed. "I'm not going to. Rachel was only making an inquiry."

***

Rachel inserted the key and pushed open the door to Lomond Lodge, indicating for Jess to go first. "That was so wonderful, to see so many badgers in one night and so close. Thank you for letting me go with you." The big brown eyes were wide and excited, and Jess grinned to herself yet again. She was initially upset with her uncle for telling Rachel about her badger watch and then more or less insisting she take Rachel along. Time alone with Rachel was something she wanted to avoid. Why? she thought. She'd enjoyed every minute of it. The tension of the last week had dissolved quickly with time spent together. She'd also found that she'd missed her badger watches these last few years by not being around in the summer, and it was good to have someone to share it with.

Their patience had been rewarded with the sighting of a large boar and an hour's entertainment by a group of cubs. The night had been still, so they had placed themselves at the bottom of the hill that housed the set. Unable to smell Rachel's familiar scent or even soap, she was disappointed yet pleased she had been taken seriously about how important it was, "Not to smell human." Mesmerized by Rachel's eyes and how they expressed her wonderment, Jess couldn't help being excited by what she had grown to take a little for granted.

Rachel hung up their coats. "There's wine in the lounge. I'll be there in a minute. I want to take the covers off the food."

She smiled as she took a glass from Jess. "Thank you again." She paused. "It was good to spend that time with you. I've missed it." Turning to place her wine on the table, she added jovially, "You always know how to show a girl a good time. I'm hungry, are you coming?"

Jess followed. "You don't have that long before you go home do you?" She instantly felt a rush of sadness at her words and knew exactly how long it was. *Six days.* "Are you still coming back? With the book signing being November." Her heart began to race as she waited on the answer.

"I'm not entirely sure yet. But I'm very much hoping to. Scott's sorting out my schedule." Jack had asked Rachel the same question yesterday. She really didn't want to think about leaving, even though she was looking forward to her sister's wedding.

Jess was disappointed in the reply. Was Rachel having second thoughts? She wasn't quite sure.

"I've grown very fond of Jack and I…" Rachel looked at Jess. "Sorry."

"It's okay. I know he's hoping you'll be back at some point." She wanted to add that she hoped she would be too.

They chatted away more easily once settled back in the lounge, occasionally wandering out for more food. The evening passed with both women relaxing just as they had done through most of the summer.

Jess eased herself back into the chair and listened intently to the melodious voice recalling some of the funnier moments of her sister's first and very short marriage when she was sixteen. They had eloped due to the fact their mother didn't like the boy, and it had been annulled on "unconsummated" grounds. Little did their mother know her sister had lost her virginity to him more than a year earlier. The marriage had never been mentioned in front of their mother again.

She watched as Rachel gestured with her hands and tossed her head back as she laughed. She then dreamily scanned every contour of her face and neck. Slowly her eyes drifted lower, reaching a cleavage that just hinted at what was below. Her mind was slowly beginning to betray her as she took in the soft mounds and then the slight swell of her belly and hips. She had a womanly shape, a total contrast to the skinny young women and the butches her own age, who hung out in the bar. She sighed contentedly. *She is beautiful. So, so, beautiful.*

Rachel continued to talk as she watched the unguarded attention Jess was showing her. The eyes had traced a lazy trail around and down the length of her body and it had unashamedly responded. That unmistakable look she had seen so often caused a wave of heat to wash over her, which instantly resulted in a moist, fluttering sensation at the top of her thighs that cried out for attention.

The eyes suddenly met hers and the red-hot piercing look she received could have melted her, if such a thing was possible. Suddenly, the intensity of the moment was over as Jess slowly blinked twice, shook her head, and rose. For some reason Rachel imagined she would be silently taken by the hand and led to her bedroom.

"I think I'd better go."

It took Rachel what seemed like minutes to register what she had heard. "Go. No." She scrambled up out of her seat and moved to within inches of Jess. Taking her hands, she softly said, "No. Please don't go. Stay. Stay with me tonight." Her heart began to thump wildly as she waited.

Blood was gushing like a torrent through Jess's head, crashing against the sides. Her eyes saw only silver flashes of light and the legs that usually carried her had definitely turned to jelly. She had to gain some sort of control and fast, but both her mind and body were playing the traitor. Through the haze she then heard the words. "Please come to bed with me, Jess?"

Rachel closed the gap completely, putting a hand to the back of Jess's head and then looked at her. Jess let out a ragged deep breath. Her head spun. "No. No I can't, I don't want to hurt you."

Rachel dropped her hand and took both of Jess's in both of hers. "You won't hurt me."

Jess desperately tried to focus and gain at least some measure of control. "You don't understand, I will. Please don't ask me again. I don't think I could help myself."

Rachel was way beyond reasoning. She had to know what it would be like to have that desire lavished on her body. "Please, Jess, I want you to touch me. I need you to touch me, please."

Jess could feel her resolve withering fast, her mind and body now in a fierce battle. "It would only lead to pain, I really should go."

Jess made a feeble move to turn away, but Rachel looked her in the eyes. "I want you, Jess. I want you to want me. I can't stand it any longer, the way you look at me. Please stay."

Jess couldn't think about anything but wanting this woman. With her body on fire and every nerve ignited, she lowered her head, put an arm around Rachel's waist and pulled her firmly against her. The feel of Rachel sent her spiraling over the edge.

Their lips met. Jess couldn't get close enough; her hands were pressing and roaming over Rachel's back and buttocks. Her shirt was being pulled and then she felt a hand on her skin. Jess groaned.

Finally, Rachel pulled away, panting and gasping for breath. "The bedroom," she said and grasped a hand that followed without protest.

As Rachel reached the bed she went for the shirt again. She gasped at the unveiling. "Oh Jess, you're as magnificent as I'd imagined." She cupped a breast and pulled Jess down for another heated kiss.

It was Jess who pulled away this time, and caressed her face. Strangely Rachel felt relaxed, even loved by the look she was receiving from that gaze that penetrated so deeply. Jess smiled and slowly leaned down to capture her mouth again. The kiss was gentle, languid and sensuous. Rachel was lost, she could only feel, not think. It was pure ecstasy. A tongue requested entry and she welcomed it with soft teasing strokes. Slowly her clothes were peeled from her body, the soft lips and agile tongue never left her.

Guiding Rachel back on the bed, Jess gloried in the body beneath her. "You are so beautiful. You can't imagine how glorious you are."

Rachel was intoxicated by such open admiration, no one had ever looked at her like that before and she needed this woman to make love to her, right now. "Jess, please?"

Jess smiled, looking down amazed at the wanting and need in those eyes. It had to be satisfied and she was going to do exactly what Rachel wished for, over and over again.

***

The pressure started to build again and Rachel's head was

spinning. *I'm going to explode.* "Just once more," she heard Jess whisper. Those same three words were said two orgasms ago and she was heading for another and her body couldn't wait. She had never experienced such pleasure.

Jess sensed the rising in the wondrous body that was driving her beyond crazy. She had never wanted to please a woman so desperately. Her tongue slowly stroked around nipples, while her fingers danced tantalizingly up and down warm moist thighs. As Rachel began to buck and sway, Jess pressed her thigh between Rachel's and pushed her center in rhythm against the movement of the woman beneath her. Instantly she was greeted with a deep guttural moan.

"You are so gorgeous. I could do this all night." Those words tickled Rachel's ear, arousing her further and causing her to push with a greater need. She felt fingers slide inside, sending her so close to the edge. They tried to slow her urgency, moving in and out in unison with Jess's thigh.

Rachel started pushing harder. "Oh yes, yes. Please I have to…"

As Rachel continued to rock, Jess slid her fingers out and then in once more while her thumb rubbed over Rachel's engorged clitoris. She cried out and dug her fingers into Jess's back, holding on, riding the wave of ecstasy washing over her. One last cry of Jess's name and Rachel collapsed, exhausted.

***

Jess stretched out on the bed with Rachel's head cradled in her shoulder, their limbs all entwined and bodies glistening with sweat. The heat they radiated left no need for the sheet that lay in a tangled heap at the foot of the bed.

"How do you do that?"

Hearing a sniffle to Rachel's voice, Jess rose and rolled onto her side. "What's wrong?"

"Nothing. Absolutely nothing. I'm happy, believe it or not." She smiled lovingly. "Nobody has ever made love to me like that. No one."

Another tear escaped and was gently brushed away as Jess

looked contentedly into the sparkling deep brown eyes. She smiled softly back. "That's because I lo—"

Jess suddenly stiffened and a look of disbelief cloaked her face. Pushing abruptly away from Rachel she rolled and stumbled out of bed. "No."

Rachel sat up feeling instantly dizzy. "What? What's wrong?" Panic riddled her voice.

Jess frantically grabbed for her clothes. She looked at Rachel with pure anguish and fright before fleeing from the room.

It took Rachel a number of seconds to comprehend what was happening. She scrambled frantically out of the bed in pursuit. Jess was already at the front door, trousers on, only half done up. Her T-shirt on back to front and rolled up over her breasts. Desperately she tugged at it as she bundled other items of clothing under the other arm.

Rachel grabbed the arm tugging at the shirt. "Jess, stop. Please stop. What have I done?"

Jess stopped only momentarily. Then pulled away and escaped through the door.

Rachel screamed, "Jess, please." She stared at the fleeing figure and then at her own naked form standing in the doorway. She closed the door before slowly sliding down the back of it, hugging her knees and sobbing uncontrollably.

***

Jess ran. She ran like she had when the lorry plowed into her family's car. She ran like she had when the logs crushed the life out of Kirsty, and she ran like she had when Alison walked into that hospital room.

Eventually, out of breath, she came to a halt aware of a painful burning sensation in her feet. She found herself in the middle of the yard, not understanding how or why she was there. Her head started to pound and a feeling of suffocation suddenly gripped her as she dropped to the ground clasping her feet.

Crawling into the barn, gasping for breath, she propped herself up against a lump of wood. Her breathing began to steady and her feet throbbed. She tried hard to think, but everything was a jumble. She couldn't understand what was happening, how long she had been here. Then to her agonizing dismay, her mind started to recall parts of what had happened. Her head fell into her hands. "Oh no, what the hell have I done?" She swallowed back the scream and blinked back the tears that welled. "Oh how could you? What sort of monster are you?"

Distraught with revulsion, anger and guilt, she couldn't gather any comprehensible thoughts. *I should go back, yes. But what do I say...Sorry?* Laughing bitterly she grabbed the ax aggressively from the wall and began to chop frantically at the wood waiting to be spliced into fire logs.

***

Waking to a feeling of dread, Jack eased himself up onto his elbow and looked around to orient himself. "Well, I'm still alive." He queried as to why he felt so uncomfortable. "I must have been dreaming." Listening, he tuned into a rhythmic noise. "That's someone chopping wood." Frowning, he looked at the illuminated display of his bedside clock. "At this time?"

Jess swung the ax down hard to meet the wood. Something was definitely wrong; if the time hadn't given it away, the appearance of his niece certainly did. She was a mess and didn't even have her boots on. "Jess?"

She stopped at the sound of her name, exhaustion instantly washing over her, she leaned on the ax embedded in the wood and stared at her uncle.

Jack waited until she slumped down heavily and sat. He inched forward dragging a small lump of wood with him and sat within inches of her. "What's going on, Jess?"

She looked at her uncle. "I need to disappear for a couple of days."

Jack was unnerved. Jess only went on walkabout if she was truly upset. He sighed. "All right, there isn't anything that couldn't wait or somebody else couldn't do."

Jess smiled without emotion. "It must be light by now?"

He'd learned many years ago, that it was fruitless pushing Jess into talking, she just distanced herself more. But looking at the pain in her eyes, he had to ask. "Yes it is, just. What's happened, Jess?"

She fought back tears again and lowered her eyes. "I've done something no one could ever forgive. An incredibly hurtful and unbelievable thing."

He looked at the head dropped in shame and knew at once that something had gone horribly wrong and it involved Rachel. Gripping her knee he replied, "Surely it can't be that bad. Would you like to talk about it?"

Jess shook her head forcefully.

"Okay. At least let me look at those feet before you go. You won't get very far if they're as bad as they look."

CHAPTER EIGHTEEN

Jess stood on the ridge overlooking the village. There was no activity out on the road, only a number of lights indicating that life was beginning to stir behind closed doors. Dawn had broken, yet the sun had not reached the top of the hill. Her sight honed in on the shop: the daily newspapers had already arrived and the van that appeared with fresh produce was parked outside.

She'd been roaming the mountains for three days and nights, only stopping to pitch a tent when it became impossible to move safely. She hadn't seen a soul by avoiding the paths to the more popular Munros and Corbetts. Something that wasn't too difficult in this vast mountainous region. She thought she'd also been lucky with the weather, or unlucky. A good lashing by the elements might have done her some good.

She sat feeling racked, tired and sick, and aware of the constant throb of her feet. Sleep had eluded her and her appetite had been nothing for the amount of exercise she had asked her body to do. It was beginning to fight back. Two days she had said to her uncle, so he and Marie had probably expected her back yesterday, if not the night before, and she didn't deserve their worry. She had to go home. The time away wasn't enough. She hadn't come up with any answers as to what she should do next. All it had achieved was to make her feel even more incapable of dealing with the situation.

The guilt she'd carried for all those months after Gretchen's attempted suicide seemed inconsequential now. This was worse. "You must be the biggest bitch on this earth, Jess Brewster." How could she ever, in a million years, make up for what she had done? There was no way anyone would forgive that.

Jess heaved herself up and headed down toward the village. Maybe a good tirade from Julie would absolve enough of the guilt to see her through the next few days until Rachel left.

***

The bell to the shop tinkled as Julie started to sort the morning papers. "You're early this morning..." She looked up expecting to see Bill, who was always first into the shop in the mornings despite probably being the last into bed at night. She gasped at the sight of her friend. "Good grief, Jess, what's happened? Is it Jack?"

Jess said in a weary tone, "No it's not Uncle Jack, he's fine."

There was urgency to the soft tone in Julie's voice as she guided Jess back through the door. "Jess, go round to the kitchen. I'll meet you there."

"Tom," Julie called, "could you keep an eye on the shop? Jess is here and she looks like shit. It's not Jack, but it's something bad."

"Yes, of course."

***

Julie finally felt she had a grasp of the situation and couldn't quite equate it with her friend. "What are you going to do?"

"What can I do? It's been over three days. Would you listen to me if I tried to explain now?" She sighed heavily. "I couldn't anyway. I can't even justify it, or explain my behavior to myself. It'll just make matters worse."

"Surely she'll at least realize that you regret what happened."

Jess laughed sarcastically. "Julie, would you forgive someone if they..." she took a deep breath, "Took you so thoroughly and then ran off, before your breathing even had the chance to settle?"

Her friend sighed and looked at the despondent and reddened face. "No, but..."

Jess shook her head. "I'm a fool, I should've known better. I've hurt her and what's the point in trying to make amends? I'll only let her down again."

Julie frowned. "What on earth do you mean by that? You can't not make amends. That's heartless."

Jess snapped, "I am heartless. What I've done is heartless. Even if I make amends and by some remote chance she forgives me, what then?" She glared at her friend. "She'll just get hurt some other way, die probably." She shook her head in frustration. "Oh, I don't know. It wouldn't be fair, just to make me feel better." She saw the shock on her friend's face and her fight dissolved as quickly as it appeared. "She'll have started to deal with it all, and I should let her do it."

Julie shook her friend's arm. "What about your uncle? How will he feel if you and Rachel are no longer speaking? You have to at least try and apologize. Wasn't she planning on coming back after her sister's wedding?"

A tear trickled down Jess's cheek. "She was hoping so. That's probably highly unlikely now."

Julie stood. "No, I think maybe you're right. Leave Rachel alone, unless she confronts you, which I actually doubt. I also doubt she'll say anything to Jack."

"How do you know that?"

"I phoned yesterday and she was visiting, nothing seemed out of the ordinary. Jack didn't even mention you were away."

"Oh," was all Jess could come up with.

"Now go and get a shower. Do you have any clean clothes in that pack?"

Jess nodded.

"Go then and I'll give you a lift up to the house after I've fed you."

CHAPTER NINETEEN

Three days had passed since Jess had been dropped off by her friend. On her return, Marie and Uncle Jack had questioned her very little. The concern and worry on their faces was evident. She had thrown herself into work around the estate. Too much time had been spent enjoying herself and jobs had been put on hold. This was a fine opportunity to catch up. Sleep was still a rare commodity; it opened her mind to thoughts she wanted to forget. Eating was no longer a pleasure either, it just left her feeling nauseated.

***

Unloading logs at Rannoch Lodge Jess mulled over in her mind what to do, if anything, about Rachel's imminent departure. Hearing footsteps coming up the path, her heart quickened until she realized they didn't belong to who she hoped it would be.

"Hi Jess."

She turned around. "Hi Tom, everything all right?"

"Yes fine, I just wanted to speak to you before I saw Jack. Can you spare me about ten, fifteen minutes?"

Jess raised a quizzical eyebrow. "How about a cuppa? I have a flask and two mugs."

He smiled. "That would be great, thanks. I actually wanted to speak to you about something personal, so please don't throw it at me. Firstly though, how are your feet?"

She smiled cautiously and sat down on the porch step, handing him a mug of tea. "They're fine, on the mend now. Personal you say?"

"Yes." He shifted a little awkwardly as he sat next to her. "Julie was telling me about your incident with Rachel."

Jess froze.

"I'm only interested in your memory loss, nothing else, don't worry."

She frowned. "Memory loss. If only. I would be jumping for joy if I could forget it all."

"No, I mean your memory loss at the time. The fact you don't remember what you did." He looked at Jess and sighed. "I'm not getting this right." He attempted again. "The running and not being aware of doing it at the time."

"I don't want to pry but I hope you know I'm your friend as well as your doctor. This is important, Jess." His tone lightened. "This has happened before hasn't it? You've run before."

Jess looked at him, tears stinging her eyes. "No. Not like this."

Tom gently squeezed her arm. "I know this is different, but it has happened before, hasn't it, a long time ago? I remember Jack saying, that you ran after your family were killed."

Jess rubbed her fingers over her brow. "Yes. I ran until I was exhausted and collapsed. They didn't associate me with the crash, as it was quite a distance away from where I was found. It wasn't until later, when I started to recall things, that they made the connection. Uncle Jack thought he'd lost everyone."

"And the next time," Tom prompted.

"Kirsty, do you know about Kirsty?" Tom nodded. "I did the same after she was crushed to death. It took a while to get any information out of me. I didn't remember everything until much later."

"Jess, do you remember refusing counseling?"

She frowned, trying to think. After her family was killed it was offered but she wouldn't cooperate. "Yes. Uncle Jack took it and wished I had. I remember him saying that."

"I remember him saying that to. I'm sorry, Jess. Julie's upset she didn't see this coming and quite frankly so am I. I should have questioned all of this before."

Jess was confused. "Why would you? There hasn't been a need."

"That's where you're wrong, Jess. You haven't exactly hidden the fact you associate love with death and disaster, but none of us have taken it very seriously."

"I don't understand."

"I don't either, Jess. I'm not qualified in that department. But it sounds like your behavior is some sort of heightened emotional response. A defense mechanism, if you like. I don't know the technical term for it." Jess looked at him blankly. "Your mind and body are reacting instinctively, like it would to anything it doesn't like or want, an allergy if you like. You have no control over it. It's something that happens unconsciously."

"No one died this time though. It's never been a problem. It's never bothered me before. Gretchen nearly died. But Rachel? Why did I run from Rachel?"

Tom took her hand. "Jess, as I said, I don't fully understand, but you have fought so long to keep love at bay. Think about that. Think about what happened with Rachel."

Jess desperately attempted to assimilate what he was saying. Some of it made sense and some of it didn't. But he was right, the one thing she was certain of, *love* caused nothing but pain, so it was best to be avoided at all costs.

Jess sighed, defeated. "Are you sure that's all it is?"

Tom placed a hand on her knee. "No Jess. You have to live with the consequences of it. You can't beat this on your own." He continued when Jess looked at him without saying anything. "A friend of mine, a professor, has an interest in this type of thing and would be pleased to meet with you. She has a clinic in town, on Wednesday and Friday mornings."

Jess glared and expelled an irritated breath. "A clinic? I take it she's some sort of psychiatrist?"

"Yes, though her specialty is psychotherapy. Jess, it won't go away, and she is willing to listen and help if possible."

"You think I'm a nut?"

"I'm sorry. I don't want to upset you. And no, I'm not implying you're mad. I just wanted to let you know there is help if you wanted it. Here's her name and number, it's up to you." Tom handed her a folded piece of paper as he stood. "Thanks for the tea. I'd better be off. Jack will be expecting me."

Jess waited until he had rounded the building and then rushed after him. "Wait, Tom. This thing, will it get worse? I should never have done what I did to Rachel. It's inexcusable." She attempted a smirk to stave off the hysteria bubbling just below the surface. "And don't worry. I already know I'm mentally unstable."

Behind the bravado, confusion and pain were evident. Tom struggled against pulling her into a hug. Instead he took her hand and said, "Speak to Carla. It has to be you who makes the contact."

***

Rachel stared out of the conservatory window toward the barn. She was visiting Jack for the last time before her return to America and wondered if the woman who plagued her thoughts would make an appearance as she had on a number of occasions throughout the summer. "Not likely," she hissed to herself.

"Rachel, I'm very fond of you, I hope you are aware of that?"

Taken by surprise, she quickly turned to see Jack as he sat down. The tone indicated that this was heading somewhere. She sat next to him reluctantly.

"I'm fond of you too, Jack."

He smiled and Rachel was struck by how unwell he really did look. "Jess is my niece, but to me, she is the daughter Mary and I were unable to have. I don't like to see her so unhappy."

Rachel was angered at the observation; she was not the one to blame for all this. It was beyond her comprehension how someone could make love to her like no other and then just run as if they had made the biggest mistake of their life. The feelings of loneliness and shame of that night, as she cried huddled up naked behind the door, came flooding back.

She swallowed back the pain. Margaret had been her saving grace, reassuring her that she could hold her head high for six days, and then regroup and think more objectively with regard to her next move.

With a light laugh in his voice, Jack took Rachel's hand. "I know a man of my years shouldn't be talking to you like this. Something has happened between the two of you, that's obvious. I have no idea what it is..." He raised a questioning eyebrow. "The little information I can glean from my niece, I fear she has done you a terrible wrong."

Rachel, close to tears, looked back at Jack. He too was upset by all of this. "You could say that."

He smiled warmly. "I'm not taking sides, Rachel." Jack gave her hand a reassuring squeeze. "I know Jess prefers the fairer sex to us macho types." He paused. "And I am assuming you feel the same way." She just nodded. "I'm guessing Jess got a little too close and then ran in the opposite direction."

Rachel's head instantly snapped up and she glared. "More like bolted."

He squeezed her hand again. "Rachel, Jess wouldn't have deliberately set out to hurt you, it's just not in her nature. She is a little..." Jack stopped and sat back discouraged. "I shouldn't be telling you this, but..."

Rachel interrupted. "Then don't." She smiled, trying to defuse the situation. "It really isn't fair for you to have to explain her actions."

"Rachel, I'm not trying to justify what she has done. Jess has let very few people get close to her. The ones she has are the ones you see around her now. You are the first person I have seen her want to spend time with and enjoy being with."

Rachel was struggling to contain her frustration and anger. Her happiness this summer had been unceremoniously ripped from her by this woman. Fighting back the tears and the lump forming in her throat, she blurted, "I don't want to talk about it." But the words continued to tumble from her mouth. "She doesn't want me, she's made that perfectly clear, and I'm not about to intrude where I'm not wanted. I've done that before, and I have no intention of making myself that vulnerable again."

"I see." Jack sat back. "Will you be coming back, Rachel?"

She sighed. "I said I would the other day."

Jack looked directly at her. "I would understand if you didn't."

She smiled her thanks for the opt-out. "No, I will be back." She added, "I can't go back on a promise to Marie, she would have my hide, and I want to help if I'm able." Rachel met his eyes warmly and placed her hand over Jack's. "You have grown to mean a lot to me in the six years. I'll definitely be back."

Marie interrupted them from the kitchen. "Tom's here." Rachel stood and kissed Jack on the cheek. "I'll see you in five weeks."

***

Jess's mood had deteriorated since her chat with Tom. She'd done her utmost to be cheerful at dinner and knew she had failed miserably. She was missing Rachel so much that her whole body ached, never mind the headache that had persisted all afternoon. The possibility of not ever seeing her again was killing her, and it didn't help that Marie and Jack didn't appear confident that she would be returning.

She looked over at her uncle as he settled himself down into an armchair. He looked much more than his seventy-three years. "Are you all right Uncle Jack?"

He groaned a little as he made himself comfortable. "Yes, thank you Jess, how about you?"

"Fine."

His voice raised an octave, much to Jess's surprise. "Oh don't give me that rubbish, Jess. You run away for three days, you mope around while you're working and you're starving yourself to death. You're eating less than I am." Rolling his eyes he attempted to add more calmly. "And another thing, young lady, you look like you haven't had a decent night's sleep in days."

Jess smiled weakly. "I'll survive."

His irritation was growing. "That may well be the case, Jess. I don't want to see you just survive. I want to see you happy. I want to leave you happy."

Tears welled in Jess's eyes. *Damn, he's afraid.* "I'm not meaning to make life difficult for you." She clasped his hand. "I'm sorry. I hadn't planned for all this to happen and I certainly don't want to hurt you as well."

"You're not hurting me, Jess, only yourself. I can only guess what you've done to Rachel, but you can't just ignore her. She's leaving tomorrow and do you honestly think she is going to come back?" Jess shook her head. "Then you have to speak to her. How do you know anything, if you don't speak? You have to speak to her before it's too late."

CHAPTER TWENTY

Jess threw back the covers and roughly pulled on joggers and a T-shirt. Slipping her moccasins on she headed down to the kitchen. It was still dark, she was exhausted and sleep, as usual, had eluded her. The "shall I, or shan't I" talk to her had played around in her head all night.

An owl began calling while she made herself tea, so she decided against the observation room and made for the back door and the porch. As she passed the utility room she grabbed a jacket and torch, trying not to spill the hot liquid. Leaning against the rail she looked out into the darkness, relaxing a little as a female owl joined in creating a soothing twit-twoo. Suddenly shards of light flickered through the trees. Surprised,

Jess frowned trying to work out what someone might be up to. Then she realized. Car headlights and they were moving from the direction of Lomond Lodge. *Rachel.*

Jess vaulted over the railing and ran toward the yard. Reaching the open space she snatched the torch from her pocket. Heading down the path through the woods she hoped she could intercept her further down the track.

Please, please let me catch her on the first bend. It was dangerous to be running through these woods at night and her feet...*Ignore your feet. Moccasins, what a fool.*

***

Rachel started up the Jeep and pulled away from the lodge. Originally she had planned to leave around seven, but there was no point in hanging about for another three hours or more. The Jeep had been packed the evening before and there was a four-hour drive ahead of her, a couple of good breaks along the way would be better.

The sadness that had engulfed her last night threatened again. Crying herself to sleep, she thought of the possibility that Jack may not be here when she returned. She knew she was making excuses, he would be here. It was Jess that was breaking her heart. Last night was Jess's last chance to come and see her and she never appeared. *Forget it Rachel.*

Shifting into second gear to take the bend, something dashed out of the trees and onto the track. Slamming on the brakes she skidded briefly before bringing the Jeep to a halt. Whatever it was, it wasn't anywhere to be seen. Rachel froze. She was sure she hadn't hit it. Maybe it ran back into the woods. She peered over the steering wheel, afraid to get out.

Jess was lying on the ground, tires inches away from her. *She really is going to be impressed with you now.* Crawling around to the driver's side she heaved herself up.

Rachel caught a glimpse of something to her right and screamed.

The door swung open and Jess winced as she jumped back.

Rachel glared at her. "What on earth are you doing? You frightened me to death."

Jess said the first thing that came into her head. "Why are you leaving so early?"

Rachel looked at her in disbelief. "What!"

Jess stared, went to open her mouth, but nothing came out.

Rachel continued. "I could have killed you, you idiot."

Suddenly everything hurt Jess so much; her feet, ankle, knees, hands, head and her heart. Tears involuntarily spilled from Jess's eyes. "I'm sorry Rachel, I'm sorry for everything. I truly am." She dropped her head, sighed heavily and turned around, starting to limp away.

Rachel stared at the retreating figure. "Wait. You can't just say that and go."

Jess stopped and shuffled gingerly to face her. "I don't know what else to say, I don't know how to explain without making things worse."

Rachel got out of the car. She was stuck for words as well, and all the scenarios of what she would say failed her. Looking closely at Jess she shook her head. "You look terrible."

"Thanks." She looked into Rachel's eyes trying to search for something, not knowing what. Then without thinking she said, "You look as gorgeous as ever."

Anger flared instantly in Rachel. "You think a nice kind word makes everything all right? Do you know how I felt when you left me that night? I…" Rachel shook her head in frustration. "You avoid me for days and wait until the last possible minute and throw yourself under my wheels. Do you really expect a sorry and a charming word will make everything okay for when I return? Is that it?"

Jess thought desperately, trying to assimilate what Rachel had said and not said. It seemed imperative that her reply was the right one. "You're coming back?"

Rachel wanted to slap her. Instead she shook her head. "Of course I'm coming back. Though not for you."

Jess nodded. "For Uncle Jack? I understand. I told you I would only make things worse if I spoke to you and I have. I never set out to cause you any harm at all. I won't pretend I know exactly how you felt that night, I'm not you. I only know how I would feel. Used, abused, humiliated, confused and devastated that someone who appeared to care so much could do what they did."

Rachel stared at her, saying nothing. She couldn't disagree with any of it. Jess pressed on. "I avoided you, imagining the damage I would have caused and not wanting to add to that pain any further. When I saw the headlights though—I had to apologize before you left our lives forever. I truly never meant to hurt you."

Rachel was struggling against the tears, brushing them away as they trickled down her face. She couldn't talk about this now. She found it difficult to croak out what she did say. "Maybe we could talk when I get back?"

Jess nodded and instinctively replied. "I'd like that. Think only of yourself, what's important to you. I won't pester you. I'll wait until you're ready."

Swallowing hard, Rachel stammered. "Thank you." Then quickly turned and jumped back into her Jeep.

Jess muttered softly as Rachel disappeared from view. "Please drive carefully."

***

Returning to the house, Jess bathed, treated her feet and grazes best she could and iced her ankle. She felt better, the food had helped for the first time in a while, yet everything still throbbed. She'd decided on rest today, no matter what.

Jack watched her as she clattered about the kitchen. "Are you going to tell me what I've done, or do I have to guess?"

"Done? I don't know what you're talking about."

Jack grinned. "Come on, spit it out. I've done something. You're acting like a big kid."

Jess glared in her uncle's direction. "Rachel's coming back."

The grin turned into a smile. "Ah. You've spoken to her then?"

"Yes, after I attempted to kill myself under the wheels of her Jeep."

That wiped the smile from his face and instantly she felt guilty for her bad mood and sarcasm. "Yes, I've spoken to her." She attempted to look happier, but failed miserably.

"Did you apologize and explain?"

She slumped down in a chair. "If it can be classed as an apology when you're driven to it several days after it should have been given." She lowered her head in shame. "You brought me up better than that. I just don't know what's happening to me."

Jack squeezed her arm. "I think you're just having a few mid-life crises."

She smiled. "Well I might have apologized. I now have to work on my explanation. That's if she wants to hear it."

He winked. "She will."

"I hope you're right."

CHAPTER TWENTY-ONE

Five weeks later

"Rachel, welcome back." Marie greeted her with a welcoming smile and a hug. "It's good to see you, how was the wedding?"

"It was wonderful, thank you Marie, it was a super day. It was lovely to see all the family. We don't get together very often." Stepping sideways from the embrace, Rachel indicated behind her. "Let me introduce Margaret."

"Hello Marie, it's a pleasure to finally meet you."

"Likewise. Rachel talks of you often."

Rachel then inquired into Jack's health and was saddened to hear that she would notice a further change in him.

They were invited to dinner. Marie smiled at Margaret, saying, "There will be a few of us, Don, Jean, Julie, Tom, Jack,

Jess, me and possibly Bill, so please don't feel obliged to come after all your traveling." Looking at Rachel she added, "Jess will be doing the catering, so even if you decide at the last minute, just let me know. That girl could cook for a group of twenty if they just turned up out of the blue."

Rachel smiled, knowing there was no exaggeration to the statement. "We'll let you know as soon as possible, thanks Marie."

Once out in the yard, Margaret said, "I thought you looked forward to those first night dinners?"

They climbed into the Suzuki, Rachel's usual choice of vehicle when at the lodges, although she had to admit the Jeep had grown on her. "That's a lot of people you haven't met and it has been a tiring few days."

Margaret buckled her seat belt. "Oh please, Rachel, when have you known me to shy away from meeting new people? Especially ones I've heard so much about."

Rachel laughed at her friend. "And are curious about? You are just dying to set eyes on Jess, to see what I've got myself into such a frenzy about. I'll go and let Marie know we'll be there."

***

Jess stood, looking desperately into her wardrobe. The meal was all prepared, seeing to itself in the kitchen, and she could hear Jack and Marie chatting happily away to Don and Jean.

She muttered impatiently, "Come on, Jess. It's only dinner, just put something on." She decided on a pale green polo shirt. "Keep it simple, that's probably best." It went well with her black Levi jeans and dark boots. Her red curly hair remained a little unruly and combing her fingers through it she decided a cut might be in order. Looking at herself in the mirror she wondered what Rachel would see.

Once Rachel had left for the States, she'd had a choice. Either continue to wallow in self-pity, making her and everyone around her miserable, or do something about it.

After contacting Carla, she had managed to arrange a number of meetings over the last five weeks. She was acutely interested in Jess's "flight behavior," as she called it, excited even,

Jess had thought. She remembered laughing sarcastically when Carla stated, "It isn't really the problem though." That was the reason Jess was there and wondered at that moment why she had listened to Tom. It wasn't until later that Jess began to understand what Carla had actually meant. "It's just a reaction," she had said and reminded Jess that she hadn't thought it a problem until *that night*. Memory loss or the blanking out of traumatic events was not uncommon either, so Jess really was beginning to wonder why she was there at all.

She'd had to relive painful memories and started with the day when she and her family were traveling up to Scotland. She had been desperate for a pee and they were making her wait. She had whined, "If you loved me you would stop." It was after finding a quiet spot to relieve herself she witnessed the lorry career into the back of, and over, their parked car. Her mother and younger brother disappeared between them and her father and aunt had still been inside. Everything was crushed in seconds.

Carla had said, "You did what any child does naturally when they're upset or scared. They run, or hide, if they are able to."

Jess had refused counseling at the time. Thinking that all she deserved was punishment for what she had done, not help. She was convinced if she hadn't said those words they would still be alive. It didn't really matter that she recognized the picnic spot as one of their usual breaks on the trip, that they had congratulated her for hanging on as long as she had and that it was the lorry driver that caused their deaths. It was still her fault.

Carla became a little more animated at this point, and Jess was pleased to see the woman was actually human. She lectured that it should have been enforced, given the circumstances. Adding, "Children reveal much when they think they are not co-operating. You just need to spend time with them." Jess cursed her nine-year-old self for refusing help.

She had returned home that night despondent, and that had only been her second session. She then began to realize that she could quite easily have gone through life without any further problems. Except for Kirsty. She recounted Kirsty's accident to Carla. The two of them were out hiking for the day and had stopped to eat their sandwiches. While Jess was getting hers out of her backpack, Kirsty climbed a nearby log pile and then shouted to the world her love for Jess. Jess immediately told her to climb down as the logs were unsecured. There was even a warning sign of the danger. Kirsty, however, was a law unto herself. She was always reckless and disobeying of rules, a trait Jess adored. Jess, on the other hand, always did as she was told and it was just before they were about to leave that Kirsty kissed her and asked if she would pick some bluebells for her. Jess had happily trotted off to collect them and it was then Kirsty decided to climb the logs again. This time they rolled, crushing her body beneath them.

The shock at seeing another horrific event triggered Jess's flight reaction. This time she was a pubescent teenager in love. This episode was fundamental in Jess's thinking that love was not a good thing. Something to stay well away from if you didn't want to see anyone die again. This Jess understood, she could have told Carla that long ago. But then it all got very complicated.

She'd had to go through the Alison and Gretchen episode. Carla had asked whether she had chosen to take another chance at love? It appeared that over time Jess had started to doubt that her love for someone was dangerous. No one else believed it. They just thought she was unlucky. "How wrong we all proved to be," she had said bitterly.

Carla agreed that they had been right. "You were right Jess. You didn't cause those deaths. Your love didn't cause those deaths. None of them were your fault." She was firm in her conviction. She did concede it was unusual for one person to experience that number of deaths so viscerally though.

Rethinking her relationship with Alison, she had wanted to believe she was in love but she knew she had fallen short. She had been cautious. "I focused on the fun and excitement, nothing else. I wanted to protect her. Or was it myself? I don't know." She had looked at Carla for the answer.

"I don't know, Jess, only you know that." Really helpful, Jess had thought at the time. But it didn't matter, someone had still suffered.

Jess had her suspicions that Alison had a partner. Yet she

couldn't understand why she, herself, would continue an affair, if that had been the case. Gretchen had been her friend and cried on her shoulder for weeks about a possible affair her partner was having.

"I should have known the damage I was causing."

"But there was doubt," Carla had said. And she was right, there was. It didn't stop Jess feeling guilty for Gretchen's attempted suicide.

Jess remembered the anxiety she experienced in that session as it went on. "I was selfish, thoughtless and stupid. It could have been avoided. If I had made some attempt, surely I could have worked out that Alison and Gretchen were connected." Her head had started to pound.

"So what did you think of their relationship?"

Jess was surprised by the question. "Shambolic. They supposedly loved each other, yet both drove the other to acts that caused a lot of suffering."

"Exactly. Their love, Jess, not yours. How many people do you love?"

"What?" Jess's heart began to race and her head just wouldn't stop thumping.

"Your uncle, Marie, Julie, friends. Nothing's happened to them."

"You're confusing me. You're confusing the issue."

"Rachel, do you love Rachel?"

Jess suddenly found it difficult to focus at all. The noise in her head was deafening, and she could feel perspiration form on her brow and hands. She stared at Carla, feeling trapped and was convinced her heart was going to stop, it was beating so fast. She then felt hands firmly pressing on her knees.

"Jess, Jess can you hear me? There's nowhere to run here, Jess."

She was suffocating and the voice was irritating her beyond belief. She then heard someone shout, "Yes, I love her and want her. But I don't want any more pain or guilt. I couldn't bear it. It would kill me."

***

After that session Jess had seriously thought about not attending the next one. Carla had obviously thought the same thing. She'd telephoned the evening before to confirm their appointment, something she had never done previously. At this session, Jess accepted that her real problem was a fear of guilt. Guilt at the words she said to her family, guilt because she believed her and Kirsty's love for each other was responsible for her death and guilt that her affair with Alison drove Gretchen to attempt suicide. Jess hadn't liked the revelation at first, saying as much to Carla, "So I don't really care about anyone but myself?"

"Now you're being ridiculous. Of course you do. How much pain have you suffered, Jess? If you didn't care for those people do you think you would have suffered?"

"Maybe not."

"Interesting, isn't it. You can beat this, Jess. Now you know what the problem is."

Jess looked at her with wide eyes. "How? I'm a complete nutter."

"No, you aren't. Believe it or not, you are a reasonable and capable person. You just need to think—"

Irritated, Jess interrupted. "Reasonable people don't act the way I did, it was unforgivable. There is no excuse." She looked searchingly at Carla. "I couldn't bear to be responsible for..." She paused, "Something happening to Rachel. It really would finish me." She lowered her head. Therapy was exhausting.

Carla placed a hand on her knee. "Jess, you haven't been responsible for anybody's death. You've had to cope with a great deal in your life. Don't belittle your ability to have lived through it." She shook her head. "Listen Jess, you know you can't change what has happened, but you can change how you react and behave from now on. Yes, you have to fight a fear, but you can overcome it. If that's want you want. If Rachel is what you want."

Jess attempted a smile. "So I just need to convince myself that my falling in love is not a deadly curse and everything will be rosy? No pain or guilt."

Carla hadn't look pleased after that little quip and had

reiterated the running still needed to be addressed, although it wasn't important in the greater scheme of things.

That was when Jess had blurted, "Not important? That's the whole problem."

"Jess, have you been giving anything any thought? It's just a response to extreme emotional situations. The last time was out of pure fear for someone you obviously love passionately and what that could lead to."

Jess twitched uncomfortably, unable to deny that it wasn't true.

"The sorts of experiences you've had are rare, believe it or not. So I'm hoping a few coping mechanisms will be enough."

Jess conceded her flight behavior had not really impacted on her life before then. It was a simple reaction to traumatic situations. Jess remembered still being confused at the end of that last session and had confessed she needed time to think it all through.

It was a number of days later that Jess had actually been lucky enough to spend a day walking with Carla, after she'd expressed a wish to see Jess one more time before Rachel's arrival. She wanted to see how Jess had actually thought things through and the conclusions she had made. Even though she had liked Carla, she was still a therapist. Yet, when they were out walking she felt more confident and relaxed. She had the impression that's what Carla had wanted to see, Jess in her own environment.

The day had resulted in reinforcing a decision to make amends for the pain she'd caused Rachel and try to explain her actions. Even if things didn't progress any further, she might be able to reclaim her as a friend. It was worth the risk. Her feelings told her that. It was just a question of whether it was too late.

***

Now, giving herself one last look in the mirror at the top of the stairs, the doorbell rang. Her heart skipped a beat, despite knowing it wasn't Rachel and her friend. She couldn't possibly have missed them wandering down the path.

"Good evening, Jess," Tom said smiling, as Julie kissed her on each cheek.

They both followed Jess into the kitchen, commenting on how wonderful the food smelled, and placed two bottles of wine down on to the counter. The doorbell went again. Her uncle called, "Jess, could you get that please?" Her feet instantly glued themselves to the floor. Julie squeezed her arm. "I'll go, just try and relax."

Relaxing now was the furthest thing from her mind, yet she had to if she wasn't going make a complete fool of herself. This was not the impression she wanted to portray to Rachel.

It wasn't long before Julie, Rachel and Margaret entered the kitchen, Rachel speaking of her sister's embarrassment when Nigel, her husband to be, dropped the ring and to his horror it bounced onto the church floor and rolled away down the aisle. All three were laughing when they looked toward Jess and Tom. Julie hung back, forcing Rachel to make the introductions. "Margaret, this is Tom and Jess. Jess and Tom, this is Margaret."

Tom smiled and stepped forward, taking her hand as he kissed her on the cheek. "Good to meet you Margaret."

"Nice to meet you too."

Jess dragged her gaze from Rachel. The room spun and her heart was beating so hard she thought it would burst out of her chest. She looked at Margaret and smiled hurriedly, thrusting out a stiff arm. "It's a pleasure to meet you." Margaret looked taken aback. Jess told herself to relax and smiled warmly. "I'll warn you now, prepare yourself for an interrogation, they all like a new face." She couldn't believe she had actually managed to form a coherent sentence and it seemed no one else did either, as they began to laugh, breaking the tension.

Tom offered to sort out the wine as Jess turned to Rachel. "Hi, I hope you enjoyed your trip?"

She responded pleasantly. "Yes thank you, I did."

"You look well." Jess actually wanted to say, *you look more beautiful than I remember.* Then take her in her arms, kiss her and tell her how sorry she was for what she had done.

"Thank you. You're looking better than when I last saw you." Rachel lifted her eyebrows.

Sensing Rachel's melancholy, Jess reached out and touched her arm. "Glass of wine?"

"Thank you."

***

Later, Rachel and Margaret walked up the hill arm in arm to the lodge, Margaret shivered and huddled closer. "What an interesting bunch. In fact, they are a lovely group of people. I thoroughly enjoyed this evening."

Rachel grinned. "Good, I'm pleased." She briefly reflected on the night. Everyone had been in high spirits and the conversation had been as easy as any night she had spent with them. Jess had initially seemed uncomfortable, and she was unsure as to whether it was embarrassment at having to appear as if nothing had happened between them, or that she had come to terms with what she had done and moved on. Rachel decided it was neither; she'd caught Jess glancing her way a number of times and that look of desire was still evident. She shook her head. How could that be? She turned to Margaret. "What did you think of Jess?"

Margaret smiled at her friend. "I hope you don't mind, I actually liked her."

Rachel returned the smile. "Why should I mind? I like her too." She sighed. "She was quiet though, wasn't she?"

"Well, you've said before she tends to be quiet when there are a number of people around."

"Yes, I suppose."

Margaret chuckled lightly and pulled Rachel closer. "She did seem terribly nervous at first, though. I think she actually had a dose of apoplexy when you entered that kitchen. I thought I was going to have to practice my resuscitation skills."

Rachel laughed and Margaret continued, "She also had great difficulty taking her eyes off you for the entire evening."

Rachel's smile was half-hearted. "You think so?"

"I know so."

CHAPTER TWENTY-TWO

Jess called out as she entered the kitchen, "Uncle Jack, are you in the conservatory?"

"Yes."

She headed to the doorway. "I've had to take Marie to Bill's, so I will just..." She popped her head in and stopped. "Oh, my apologies, I didn't realize you had company." Jess managed an awkward smile in Margaret and Rachel's direction. "Hello." Then looking at the feast laid out she turned to her uncle. "I can see you don't need me to fix lunch."

Jack waved toward a chair. "Are you just going to stand there, or are you going to join us?"

Jess glanced over at Rachel. "I don't want to intrude."

He pulled out the seat nearest to him. "Nonsense, they have made enough for you as well."

Jack handed her a plate and the selection of sandwiches. She stacked what she thought was a polite pile onto her plate and sat back. Jack continued. "We were just discussing Rachel's book signing."

"Oh yes?" She glanced at Rachel again. She was having a little difficulty not looking her way.

"Jack's decided he would like to attend the party."

She placed her plate down and turned to her uncle for confirmation. "I've not been to a good party in years. Rachel invited us all the other night at dinner, and it appears we're definitely the only ones that can go."

Jess's eyes widened as she sat forward again. "We?"

Jack patted her knee and smiled. "Yes, you and me."

She looked from Rachel to Margaret and then back to her uncle. Rachel smiled. "Yes."

Jack looked triumphant. "All sorted then. I'll organize the transport and the hotel."

Jess sat back again. "Okay then."

After a moment he asked, "Are you not going to argue with me?"

She smiled without flinching. "No, why?" She desperately wanted to argue and tell them what a damn stupid idea it was. He didn't have the strength or the stamina for a weekend in London. But who was she to deny him if that's what he wanted?

Margaret said, "I did offer to put you both up, but Jack wouldn't hear of it."

"Thank you Margaret, a hotel is probably more practical."

Jess agonized for the rest of lunch and during the clearing up afterward. She needed to speak to Rachel. It was highly unlikely she would really want her at the book signing. It was going to be an important and difficult enough day as it was.

After they said their goodbyes to Jack, Jess followed the two women out the front door. Jess took the plunge. "Sorry, Rachel, could I have a quick word, please?" Rachel stopped. Margaret moved a few feet away. "About the book signing. If you would rather I didn't go I…"

She interrupted Jess curtly. "Why wouldn't I want you to go? I don't make invitations I don't mean." She quickly turned and strode toward Margaret, who raised an eyebrow at her in question. She stopped, sighed and returned to speak to Jess. "I'm sorry, that was uncalled for but..."

Jess continued for her. "But you have enough to deal with at the moment. And now the book signing with Michelle will include me being there. Fantastic, eh?" Rachel's eyes widened. *Bingo*, Jess thought. She persevered. "Believe it or not, I do have some say in what I do and don't do. I could easily get out of it."

Rachel smiled and said, "I may have fought this venture all the way, but I'm beginning to see how right Scott was. I would very much like to have you both there." She smiled again.

Jess thought she was going to get her head bitten off for putting words into Rachel's mouth, but the words were sincere. Waves of electricity rushed through her body as she met Rachel's eyes.

CHAPTER TWENTY-THREE

Finishing her coffee as she and Margaret watched the birds feeding, Rachel asked, "How did you get us into a whole day with Jess?"

"How could I resist a tour of the rugged countryside with a rugged woman? I didn't think you'd trust me."

Rachel rolled her eyes. "You wouldn't do that to Diane."

Margaret winked. "Six weeks apart is a long time." Diane had returned to her native New Zealand to spend time with her sister who had three children under the age of six and twins on the way. To make matters worse, their mother had been involved in a road traffic accident that had left her with a fractured leg and ribs. So Diane, rather than worry from a distance, was more than willing

to help. Unfortunately, she and her mother had never seen eye
to eye and she certainly didn't approve of her relationships with
women. Usually, that wouldn't deter Diane taking Margaret with
her. This time though, they thought for everyone's comfort she
would stay behind.

They sat quietly for a few moments before Margaret said,
"You seem much more relaxed in Jess's company. I didn't think
you'd mind. She said we needn't go if you were uncomfortable
about it."

Rachel looked at her friend suspiciously. "What are you
getting at, Margaret? And why would Jess feel I might be
uncomfortable?"

"Well, it's certainly a possibility. You still don't trust her do
you?"

"Did Jess say that?"

"No. I've just said it. I can understand that you wouldn't. I
wouldn't want my feelings thrown back in my face again either."

Rachel frowned. That's all she had thought about since she'd
come back. What would happen if she let Jess into her heart
again? She was finding it difficult to think beyond those desolate
feelings of being deserted like that. If it happened once it could
happen again. Yet she was in danger. She liked Jess. She was a
wonderful, thoughtful and humorous woman to be around. She
shook her head and sighed.

Margaret looked at her. "Rachel, I find it difficult computing
Jess with the woman who deserted you. She's besotted with you.
It's written all over her face."

Rachel suddenly stood. "Do you think I dreamt it? Made it
all up? I'm finding this difficult as well. I can cope with things the
way they are now. If…"

Margaret grabbed Rachel's arm. "I'm sorry Rachel. I know.
Please sit down?"

Rachel sat, looking at her friend. "I'm sorry, too." It seemed
recently, that whenever they discussed Jess, it resulted in an
argument.

Margaret patted her knee. "Let's not spoil the day. She'll be
here shortly. Come on, let's get ready."

***

Jess pulled up the Range Rover in front of Lomond Lodge, switched off the engine and climbed out. It was a beautiful still day, a little cold, but perfect for the short walk and leisurely day she had in mind.

Rachel emerged, smiling. "Good morning. Just waiting for Margaret."

"No hurry." Jess stood, not able to help her eyes scanning the entire length of Rachel's body. She looked so relaxed and beautiful, the khaki jeans and white T-shirt fitted comfortably to every curve and contour of her body. Her hair shone in the sunshine and those big brown eyes were bright.

Recognizing the look, Rachel stopped, and swallowed as her mouth instantly dried. Instinctively she licked her lips to moisten them as she peered dangerously into those eyes. She watched them dilate causing other areas of her body to treacherously moisten. *Oh great. This is getting more difficult.*

"Morning, Jess." Margaret slapped Rachel on the back as she bustled past her. "Come on Rachel, lock up. I've got the bags and your jacket."

Jess cleared her throat and smiled. "Hello, Margaret. You're all set then?" Quickly turning she opened the doors to the Range Rover.

***

"I can't believe that noise. They must be hoarse by the end of the day." Margaret looked at Jess. "I thought you said it was peaceful in the mountains?"

Rachel and Jess laughed. "It is. You can't hear anything else can you?" Jess replied. "I'll go and get the sandwiches."

Rachel reached out. "Jess, could you bring my bag in please?" Jess smiled and nodded as she left the hide.

"This place really is incredible, Rachel. Are you sure you don't want to get any closer? Jess said it would be all right."

"No this is perfectly fine. It's the landscape I'm more interested in at the moment. These telescopes will do the trick if I want more detail. And it's warmer in here than out there for lunch. I thought the bellowing was bothering you anyway, it'd be worse if we were any nearer."

Margaret chuckled. "It's not really. I just never imagined deer were so vocal, and it carries. You hear them way before you see them."

"Just the stags," Rachel teased. "I've never heard it before either. I'm usually away by the rutting season."

"So you're an expert now, after our little talk?" They both grinned as Jess walked back in.

Margaret took the lunch box. "I'll sort this out."

Rachel took her bag from Jess and smiled. "This is wonderful. You were right about the light. The colors are so rich and vivid, and the mountains so well defined. It really is beautiful."

Jess was pleased. "The light is always different at this time of the year. It's clear and clean, like nowhere else." She chuckled. "That I've been anyway."

"You mean when you can see it through all that rain you have up here. Not forgetting the mist and fog."

Rachel turned around. "Margaret, the weather's been pretty good since you've been here."

She grinned. "That's what I mean." She looked at Jess. "Seriously though, Rachel is right, it is beautiful."

While they tucked into their lunch, Rachel got out her watercolors. There was so much she could capture. The scenery was vast with burns snaking their way across uneven ground of grasses, rock and carpets of moss. Rowan trees covered large areas, their berries producing a blood red haze at the base of the hills. The bright orange and browns of the dying bracken dotted about in magnificent swathes. And the dark green expanse of the pine forest next to the grays of the open mountain sides. It was dramatic. She couldn't help but smile when she looked at the herd of deer and the great stag, with his antlers magnificently branching on his head. It was a scene very reminiscent of many traditional Scottish paintings she had seen.

Jess became conscious she was staring at Rachel. She could watch her paint all day. This waiting for Rachel to question her about what happened was getting increasingly difficult.

"Jess." She turned toward Margaret. "Those are mountain hare aren't they?"

Jess looked to where she was pointing. "So you were listening this morning then?"

"I most certainly was. I enjoyed that little guided walk. It may have been a bit hilly, but I'm getting better at tackling them. Rachel said you worked as a guide for a holiday company?"

"I did."

"You should do them from the lodges. I'm sure you'd have a lot of takers for the sort of walk we did this morning. It's nice to know what you're looking at, or just walked by for that matter."

Rachel laughed. "I think Jess has enough to do."

"Rachel's right. I don't mind doing it for certain people. I'm more possessive of the wildlife around here and besides, there are quite a number providing the service already. Mainly the bigger treks though."

"Jess, that won't sell it to Margaret. If you want her to bring Diane up here for a couple of weeks, you'll have to do better than that."

"Ah, well then. If you were to come in the summer, I might be able to provide a couple of exclusive short walks. I can also provide very detailed maps."

"Oh, I can vouch for those. You get to see some hidden treasures with those." Rachel winked at Jess before turning back to her painting.

Clearing her throat, Jess continued. "There are numerous sites of historical interest for the more intellectual visitor; burial grounds, battlefields and castles. Rocks and grass to some people." Margaret and Rachel laughed. "The highlight, if you don't fancy any of the numerous outdoor activities yourself, is to watch other people exert themselves at our local highland games in August."

Rachel interrupted. "Yes, they are always worth a visit. Tossing the caber, tug-of-war, chasing pigs and playing the bagpipes, all done in the rain and mud."

"I think that's a slight exaggeration," Jess said, grinning.

"No it's not. I have been every year and it's rained. It's been a lovely day, but it's rained."

Jess shook her head. "It was glorious this year. T-shirt and shorts weather. You need to try again."

"Maybe I will."

Jess really hoped that she would. "Anyway back to my selling."

"It's okay, Jess. I'm already sold."

***

It was an hour or so later when Rachel put down her brush. Jess and Margaret had chatted away, leaving her to paint. They'd even disappeared for a short time, and Margaret came back excited at seeing a golden eagle. Every bird of prey to Rachel was either a kestrel or a buzzard, unless Jess was there to point out the differences. She'd learned more this summer about the lodges, the area and the wildlife than the other six years put together. She glanced back at Jess and swallowed down a hard lump that was lodging itself in her throat. *Stop it.* She listened as she gazed out of the window and it seemed every question Margaret had, Jess knew the answer. There was no arrogance in her knowledge, just a love of the area and a willingness to pass it on to anyone who wanted to know. She sighed. The day really was beginning to remind her of the many she and Jess had shared in the summer. She concentrated as the stag started to hurry through his harem of does, attempting to round any loose ones up and then jump up onto a prominent rock and start to bellow. Trying to get the telescope set on him proved impossible. She was seeing everything but the stag.

"Can I give you a hand? There must be another stag in the vicinity. That's why he's up there, showing the intruder who's boss."

Rachel looked up at Jess, her attentive stare bore right into Rachel. She stammered, "I can't focus it." Jess bent down to look through the eyepiece and then reached for the focuser and caught Rachel's hand still resting on the telescope. Goose bumps instantly traveled throughout Rachel's body. She felt her nipples harden and her center pulsate. She quickly whipped her hand away and clutched the bench to steady her swaying head.

Jess trembled as she attempted to focus the telescope. Her legs were in great danger of giving way. "They are not as easy to handle as binoculars." She gripped onto the eyepiece hoping to defuse the heat that was racing through her body. One fleeting touch of Rachel's fingers was all it took and her body was a roaring flame. Focusing on the noise of the roaring stag she eventually got him into focus and pulled away to steady her gait. She looked at Rachel. "Beautiful—the stag. The stag is beautiful." Jess stepped back to give Rachel room and bumped into Margaret, quickly sobering her. "Sorry."

Rachel stood, needing to hold onto something. She was conscious that if she grabbed the telescope, Jess would need to refocus it. She wavered attempting to look through the eyepiece.

"Here, put your hand up here." Rachel was suddenly very aware of Jess's close proximity again and her scent wafting her way wasn't helping either, but luckily her casual manner was. She placed her hand where instructed and focused. It also helped when she heard Margaret say, "Can you see it?"

After a moment she replied, "Yes, it's magnificent. Oh yes, Margaret, take a look."

Rachel picked up her sketchpad as another stag came into view.

***

A few hours later, Margaret flopped herself down into the armchair. "I'm exhausted. And I can't believe I've volunteered to help Jess with her chores one day." She laughed. "To take a quote from someone not too far away, that woman sure knows how to show a gal a good time."

Rachel smiled, she couldn't disagree. Today had been a struggle, but she couldn't deny she'd enjoyed it and if she thought about it, could feel a little jealous that Margaret was going to be spending another day with Jess instead of her. It's your own choice, she thought. She sighed. "I think I'll give this to Jess." She showed Margaret a sketch of two stags with antlers locked in battle.

"I think she'd like that."

***

It was late in the evening. Jess settled next to her uncle on the settee. He had appeared to have more energy this last week, although his mobility was a little impaired. They were seeing the consultant again tomorrow and x-rays were scheduled to see if there was a cause for the decreasing strength in his legs.

"I was speaking to Rachel and Margaret about how this place came to be. Aunt Mary's excitement at seeing her dream materialize with your help."

He covered her hand with his. "If it wasn't for her, the lodges wouldn't be the place it is; she had great vision."

Jess nodded thoughtfully and it made him laugh. She turned to face him. "What?"

He smiled. "That look was very reminiscent of her. You're like her in very many ways."

Jess grinned. "That will be your influence."

He shook his head. "Oh no, you can't blame me for that. Do you remember when you and Mary were looking at the designs for the lodges? You both piped up at the same time, 'Where are the drying rooms?' Only true outdoor people would come out with a statement like that." He chuckled. "And I can't remember how old you were then." He sat contentedly and Jess snuggled closer. "She always loved it when you came to visit in the summer. It was a guarantee she would have an enthusiastic companion to drag out and about."

Jess looked up at him. "Well it must have rubbed off on you as well. I can't see you anywhere else either."

He squeezed her hand. "You're right. I couldn't imagine not having this place and you after everyone had been taken away from us." They both looked at each other, emotion in both their faces. Jess swallowed hard. "Did I stop you from talking about them?"

Jack frowned. "Where did that come from? No, never." He shook his head. "You always indulged me. I tried to involve you in discussions when I knew it was upsetting you, I'm sorry for that. I just wanted you to stop blaming yourself."

Jess rested her head on his shoulder and whispered, "I turned out all right though, didn't I?"

Jack beamed and kissed the top of her head. "You did more than all right, I couldn't have hand-picked a better niece."

They sat silently for a while before Jess quietly said, "I think Rachel's mellowing toward me a little. Well, at least tolerating me."

"I have to agree; the tension between the two of you does appear much better. You had a good day today then?"

"Yes." She chuckled nervously. "I'm going to invite her out for lunch and attempt to…explain things. I've been hoping she would ask." She added as her uncle frowned. "I said I would leave it up to her when she wanted to talk."

He nodded slowly. "Then I think that's good, Jess, a positive move. Why don't you have lunch here, on Friday? You could have the place to yourself. After my appointment with Tom, I'll have a meal at the pub with Bill and Marie."

It was Jess's turn to frown. "I was going to go with you. He'll have the results of tomorrow's x-rays."

"Don't be silly, there's no need. I'll fill you in when I get back. If you just take me into the village I'll be fine."

CHAPTER TWENTY-FOUR

Rachel walked around to the back of the reception area a little apprehensively. Jess had asked if she would have lunch with her; there were things she wanted to explain. Then, as suddenly as the invitation was made, she'd desperately added, "You don't have to. I know I said it was up to you and it is."

Rachel's reply had been instant: "I'll be there." She wanted to know what Jess meant by explaining things. Suddenly she was uncertain whether she really did want to know. She shook her head and scolded herself. "You're a grown woman for heaven's sake. This should be much easier."

Tapping on the kitchen door she took a deep steadying breath. "Hi Jess, are you there?"

Jess turned around from cutting bread. "Hello, come in." Rachel looked gorgeous as always. Jess smiled and wiped her hands on a tea towel. "Please take a seat. Lunch is actually ready. Is that okay?"

Jess joined her after laying everything out on the table, and sat back as Rachel helped herself. Looking at her own food she pushed her plate slightly forward so she could rest her elbows on the table. "I'd like to try and explain to you why what happened, happened." She looked at Rachel. "Please don't think I'm trying to excuse what I did, though."

Rachel nodded and smiled encouragement.

Clearing her throat, Jess said, "This will be hard to believe. I wasn't actually aware I'd deserted you until it was too late."

The look of disbelief she was receiving pushed her on. "One minute I was holding you, the next my feet were killing me. I was in the yard with no shoes on and only half dressed. I didn't know how I'd got there. It wasn't until later, after I crawled into the barn, that pieces of the evening started coming back to me. Even then, it took some time for me to wake up to the reality of the situation."

Rachel almost jumped out of her chair. "The situation." Her face reddened, and Jess visibly squirmed. "No one has made love to me like that, no one. I was so happy and you bolted. *Bolted*, Jess. As if you'd made the biggest mistake of your life. You left me feeling…" She sat back in her chair suddenly deflated. "Oh it doesn't matter, you know how I felt."

Jess fought back the overwhelming defeat engulfing her, but she had to get this all out now that she'd started. "It does matter."

Rachel gave out a short gasp, not saying a word. She pressed on. "I couldn't make sense of what had happened, it was all so jumbled but I did sort it eventually. And I remembered."

Her voice breaking and her eyes brimming with tears, Rachel asked. "Why didn't you come back? You could have just come back."

Jess lowered her head. "My memory, it was so slow in returning, I was desperately trying to remember exactly what had happened. I couldn't recall it quickly enough." She looked back up at Rachel trying to regain her composure. "When I did, I thought it was too late to make up for what I'd done. And I didn't have a clue how to."

"You could have started with a 'sorry.' That might have helped."

Jess sighed heavily and reluctantly said, "I was afraid to."

Though she was obviously trying to stay calm, the anger in Rachel's voice was still evident. "You avoided me for days. Surely I'm not that frightening?"

Jess swallowed hard. "I'm not explaining this well. I was scared you'd forgive me."

Rachel looked confused. "What? I don't understand."

"I was so happy, more than happy. I'd been fighting my feelings for you for months and it all felt so good." Jess took a deep breath. "I was about to tell you…" She paused and looked straight at Rachel. Anxiety started to take control, yet she managed somehow to keep it at bay. She took another more calming breath and continued. "I was about to say that I loved you, and something snapped and I panicked. I didn't want to love you." Relieved that she'd said it and that Rachel didn't utter a word, she took the opportunity to continue. "Unfortunately, it's happened to me before." She shook her head. "The panic thing I mean, not the declaration."

She waited to see if there would be a response. Nothing. "While you were away, I saw a psychotherapist. Actually she's a professor of psychiatry. Carla, that's her name. Said my running was the result of a heightened emotional response triggered by certain events."

Rachel's eyebrows knitted together. She instantly thought back to the counselor she and Michelle had seen. The one she caught her partner in bed with two years later. "Carla. Did you see her professionally or personally?"

Jess was taken aback by the question spat at her. "Professionally, I didn't know her before. I've seen her a couple of times off the couch though. She's a friend of Tom's." Her attempt at a joke hardened Rachel's features further. Jess sighed. "If you had forgiven me, I was afraid it would happen again, or something much worse."

"Worse?" Rachel shook her head in astonishment. "How long have you had this problem?"

Jess sucked in a breath at the harshness of the words. "I never saw it as a problem, until that night. The running, it hadn't really affected me before then. There's more to it, though."

Rachel stood with no expression on her face that Jess could read. Worried that she was going to leave, Jess frantically said, "Please Rachel, sit down."

The pleading in her voice was not lost on Rachel. She tried to tell herself that this woman wasn't Michelle with all her excuses. Rachel sat herself down again and waited.

Jess went on to explain the other times she'd run and how eventually she simply just avoided falling in love to prevent anyone from getting hurt, or worse, dying and more feelings of overwhelming guilt. "Unfortunately, I've gone so out of my way to avoid love that my poor simple mind couldn't cope with the prospect of it. I know it sounds strange, but when I realized what had happened, extreme anxiety and fright set in, causing me to run. I honestly didn't do it consciously."

Rachel watched Jess. The woman had been through hell. Jack had told her of the accident that had taken their family, but he'd left out the details. She also knew vaguely about Alison and Gretchen due to overheard arguments. She hadn't asked Jess the details. Kirsty, Jess had mentioned months back, but again she didn't ask anything further. *It's a wonder she isn't in the loony bin. I would be.* Then she recalled the night Jess had made love to her and her heart began to race. Was she actually in love with her? That's what she had said, but was it still true? "Is it still a problem?"

Jess smiled, relieved that she'd confessed all. "Is what still a problem?"

"Are you still in love with me?" She dreaded the answer, in case it was no.

Jess took a deep calming breath and captured Rachel's eyes with her own. "Yes." The word hung in the air for what felt like an eternity. Jess thought she might run again, quite deliberately this time though. She felt sick and suddenly very exposed.

Rachel was initially ecstatic to hear the news and then unsure whether it really was all true. The focus was now on her and she didn't like it. What did she have to offer someone like Jess anyway? What if Jess had mistaken her feelings? What if she ran again, could she deal with it? She had to regain her composure, she had to stop thinking. "Are you in danger of running from me again?"

Jess bit her bottom lip. "I don't know." Sighing she added, "What I do know is that fighting my feelings has caused as much pain as if I had just accepted them, probably worse. I can't take back how I behaved. I'm extremely sorry it happened, and I truly never meant to hurt you. All I want to do is put it right and I don't know how to. You're the last person in the world I ever wanted to hurt." Jess slumped back in her chair exhausted. "But I did."

Rachel couldn't help herself. She rose, walked over and pulled Jess into a fierce hug. Her heart started to quicken and her breathing deepened when she realized in her enthusiasm to comfort, she had placed the lips she so wanted to feel on her again, right between her breasts. Arms slowly went around her waist as Jess pulled back and rose out of her seat.

It was instant. Rachel captured roughly the mouth she needed to taste. Tongues fought and danced in desperation.

Breathless and with her head spinning, Jess was close to climaxing. Her need for this woman was uncontrolled and from just one kiss. "Rachel, I need more. You have to be sure this is what you want, or I have to walk away right now."

Rachel looked at her dumbly, her body tense with arousal. Steadying her ragged breaths she replied, "I'm sure. This time though I need to touch you."

Jess took her hand. "Anything. Come with me."

Clothes left a trail from the bedroom door to the bed. Jess looked up at Rachel who was straddling her hips, moisture from her center dampening her own mound. She so wanted to slip her fingers slowly through the soft velvet folds she could only imagine. Rarely in her life had she played the nondominant role. It scared her and excited her all at the same time. "Please Rachel?"

Rachel had been assertive so far, she was determined she would be the one in control. She felt powerful and petrified. Her thoughts betrayed her. Michelle had always made it quite clear she was a failure as a lover. If she was, Jess would find out soon enough. She floundered over what to do next. It would be so easy to let Jess take command and her aching body would be satisfied. She needed that release and so did the woman beneath her.

Rachel smiled and tossed her concerns aside. Slowly she lowered her head to the breasts so tantalizingly awaiting her touch. A nipple instantly reacted to her tongue and a groan urged her on. She licked, nipped, pulled and feasted before slowly kissing her way southward, over a taut, smooth abdomen. When she reached the glistening center so swollen and ready, the heady aroma was intoxicating, she wanted to fill Jess with herself. She needed to be inside her, give her the joy she had experienced at Jess's touch. She kissed and flicked her tongue around the soft swollen area and slowly moved back upward.

Jess could feel herself choking on her words as Rachel moved from where she most needed her. "Rachel please, I can't stand it any longer." Her body was a live wire; she could sense it writhing in all directions. Blood was rushing through her head and it felt like a pulsating hot mass that was in danger of erupting. Rachel made her way back up to her lips and she responded instinctively, hungry for any part of the woman setting her whole being on fire. Fingers fleetingly touched her needy clit before moving lower. She clutched clumsily at Rachel's wrist and managed. "Not inside." Rachel's hand then pressed hard in just the right place and her body stiffened then shuddered. Vaguely she recalled someone calling out Rachel's name as waves of pulsating pleasure washed over her body again and again.

She groaned when the body, so entwined with hers, moved away. It was impossible to coordinate mind and body, nothing happened. When she managed to orient herself, Rachel was dressing. She had no clue as to how much time had passed. Scrambling off the bed she immediately found herself lying on the floor with Rachel hovering over her.

Rachel was stunned, she was on the very precipice of orgasm when a hand clasped her wrist and denied her entry.

Had Jess grown impatient when she hadn't done the right thing? Did she guide her hand to where she wanted it? She couldn't remember.

Rachel stood, desperately trying to compose herself. No one was ever supposed to hurt her again.

"Jack and Marie will be back shortly, and I don't really want to be caught here."

Jess smiled and went to place her arms around Rachel's waist. "Why not?"

Rachel stiffened and suddenly stepped back. "I don't think it's a good idea, I will speak to you later." She quickly pulled on the rest of her clothes and headed for the door.

Jess stumbled after her. "Rachel wait." She called desperately, "Rachel, please stop. What's happened? What have I done?" There was no response. Jess stood for a moment totally confused and disoriented, then slumped onto the floor. "I love you."

***

Jess slammed the door to her bedroom and stomped down the stairs muttering, only to be met at the bottom by Marie, Julie and Jack. She looked at her uncle. Tears began to well in her eyes. It wasn't going to be good news and that's not what she wanted to hear.

Taking a deep breath, she asked, "It's not good is it?"

He smiled. "We knew it wouldn't be. There are things we need to discuss. At this moment though, I'm more interested in why you're in such a foul mood and where is Rachel?"

"It's not important. Tell me what Tom had to say." Julie followed them, while Marie went through to the kitchen to put the kettle on.

***

Jess wheeled into the barn bicycles that had just been returned by a family, ready for her to clean and check later.

Idly, Julie leaned up against a post with her arms folded and asked, "Want to talk about it?"

"I think we covered everything, didn't we? Getting a good nurse won't be a problem will it?" She knew exactly what her friend was referring to and she didn't want to discuss it. Her uncle's cancer was spreading rapidly, a new tumor had been found and either home care, or hospice care, needed to be considered in preparation.

"I meant Rachel. Your lunch obviously didn't turn out well."

She slumped down and filled her friend in, being careful to leave out the more intimate details. The part Julie always tried to prize out of her.

Her friend frowned. "What made her walk out like that? Maybe she did think it was best to leave before we arrived." She didn't look convinced. "Are you sure you didn't do something to upset her?"

"No." Jess answered, exasperated. "Not that I'm aware of, I thought everything was—perfect."

Julie ignored Jess's blush. "You didn't have a memory block or anything did you?"

"Oh for goodness sake, I'm fed up with this stupid thing. It's never been a problem before, but all of a sudden I'm some sort of head case." She flung her arms up, grumbling. "I don't think I did. I remember feeling groggy and I couldn't get my brain or body to work for a wee while, but that's it."

Julie stifled a grin. "Was that postcoital?" Jess just glared at her.

Julie put an arm around her shoulders. "I have to agree with Carla, you are a passionate creature my friend, so I think you're entitled to be a little groggy after sex. I'd be incredibly offended if Tom got up straight away and asked me if I'd like a cup of tea."

Jess couldn't help herself, she had to chuckle. "I suppose I got what I deserved."

Julie dragged her arm back and pushed at Jess's shoulder until she faced her. "What do you mean by that? She wasn't getting even, was she?"

She shook her head. "No, I don't think so. Rachel isn't that calculated."

Her friend looked at her skeptically. "You sure about that? She's not been very forgiving."

Jess blew out a breath. "I don't know. I was planning on going up and asking her what I'd done wrong." She looked at her friend for confirmation that was the thing to do.

Julie rolled her eyes. "Why don't you ask her what went wrong instead?"

***

Taking a deep breath Jess knocked confidently on the front door to Lomond Lodge. "Hi Margaret, would it be possible to speak to Rachel please?" She felt like a child asking her friend's mother if she could come out to play.

"Sorry Jess, she said she didn't want to speak to you." Her face indicated she truly was sorry.

"I was hoping to find out…Why doesn't she want to speak to me?"

Margaret sighed. "She's a little upset at the moment."

Jess bristled; she couldn't understand what was going on at all. "Well, actually, so am I. Did she give any indication when she might speak to me?"

Margaret raised her eyebrows. "No."

"I would just like to know what I did wrong. I have absolutely no idea."

Margaret stepped out onto the porch pulling the door behind her. "I'm sorry, Jess, Rachel is my best friend, and I can't jeopardize her trust. I really do wish I could help you."

Jess saw the anguish in Margaret's eyes. "Would you mind asking her to try and see Uncle Jack tomorrow afternoon? You too?" She sighed heavily. "I'll make myself scarce."

Margaret gently smiled and a placed a hand on Jess's arm. "We'll be there, and I am sorry, Jess."

She attempted to return the smile and failed miserably. Quickly turning she headed down the path fighting back the tears.

CHAPTER TWENTY-FIVE

"Fan-bloody-tastic." Margaret closed the door behind her and leaned back against it looking up at the ceiling. "Great."

Rachel emerged from the bathroom dressed in a robe. "What is it?"

Margaret walked past her saying nothing and into the kitchen. She held up a bottle of wine, to which Rachel nodded. She popped the cork and poured out two glasses. "That was Jess."

Margaret filled her in on the details of the conversation as she led the way into the lounge and sat down on the sofa.

Rachel watched her friend gaze out of the picture window, obviously waiting for a response. "Do you really think she doesn't know what she did?"

Margaret answered carefully. "Yes, and I'm not entirely sure you know either."

"What?" Rachel snapped her head in her friend's direction.

"I think Jess genuinely cares for you. Why would she give you such an explanation for her behavior? Those tragedies are not something you invent and guilt is a very powerful emotion. It could have been much simpler and not so dramatic if all she wanted was to get you into bed. As for the rest, it has to be a misunderstanding."

"Oh, so it's me as usual?" Tears welled in Rachel's eyes.

"That's not what I said, or meant. I'm sorry. Can it not all be a misunderstanding, what happened?"

Rachel rested her head back against the sofa. "I'm not convinced about that, but I may have been a little harsh. She's experienced some awful things. The whole thing's plausible, I suppose. Oh, I know it's plausible, but…"

Margaret took her hand. "Yes, I think it is."

Rachel gave a faint smile. "I think we made a mistake being more than just friends."

"What makes you say that?" Margaret rolled her eyes at her reply.

"I've had little experience when it comes to satisfying a woman." She lowered her head. "I consciously decided to take command, to see if I had what it took to be a good lover, and I failed miserably."

Margaret sighed. "Listen Rachel, why would she have gone to all the trouble of seeking help? Then patiently wait to explain it all to you if she wasn't in the least bit interested in you and thinking further than just sex?"

"The thrill of the chase and the conquest." Rachel sighed. "Oh I don't know. It's not going to work. She's now experienced the rewards and will have realized it isn't worth it."

Margaret closed her eyes, exasperated. "Speak to her tomorrow. I still think it's a misunderstanding."

"I'll speak to her."

***

Rachel wandered over to the barn. She and Margaret had just left Jack. It had been a sad half hour, Jack's mood was low and he appeared distant. He was not his usual upbeat self. His excuse was that he was tired, and Rachel thought it was understandable considering the circumstances. Yet, she had the feeling that was not the true reason and it had more to do with her.

Since her conversation with Margaret she had gone over, numerous times, her relationship with Jess and it was full of extremes. She had never experienced such joy and pleasure in another woman's arms and fun when they weren't trying to be lovers. The summer months they had spent together had been the most wonderful of her life. The depth of the heartache though, was too great. Even Michelle had never caused the level of turmoil she had experienced recently. Or had she? Rachel didn't know anymore. The best way forward she had decided was for Jess and her to remain as friends. She had worked hard the last six years to put this kind of emotional stress behind her and couldn't go through it all again. Woodland Lodges and Jack had been a part of her healing and she was grateful for that. She remembered her first short visit here after she had left Michelle and the stormy two days when Michelle had come after her. Even then, Jack had made it clear during those days that if she required any assistance that she just had to ask. No one asked questions and no one intruded. Again, the following year when she booked herself in for five months with stipulations of how she wanted the same lodge kitted out, no one grilled her, or made her feel uncomfortable. That summer she got to know the residents of Woodland Lodges.

She sighed. She did love this place and its people. It was a total contrast to the hustle and bustle of her city life, a place to recharge her batteries. No distractions, other than the scenery and her art. Even her sketching came second to her painting here and that hadn't been a bad thing, they'd improved in the last few years, along with commissions. This place had been good for her, yet coming back for another summer was not an option anymore. And if Jack was now unsettled by her presence, she would leave sooner rather than later, despite her promise to help as much as she was able. This, she really did need to discuss with Jess.

She sighed and muttered, "It won't be the same anyway. The people won't be the same." Her thoughts then betrayed her. The place would stay the same. Jess had always been here.

Jess turned around at the sound of her name and looked expectantly at Rachel, who took a deep breath as if she were going to deliver a sermon. "Jack has explained that his cancer has spread further and that's what's impeding his walking. I would like to be of help if I can, but I don't want to be in the way, or make things awkward for him or the people closest to him." Jess watched Rachel's shoulders slump as she continued. "This is a very difficult time for everyone and it shouldn't be made more so by anyone."

Jess was touched by the unguarded honesty; it reminded her of the days they had spent together, when talking seemed to be so easy. She sighed and then smiled unreservedly. "Shall we sit?"

They perched side by side on a log. "Rachel, all any of us probably want at this moment is what's best for Uncle Jack." She turned to Rachel for confirmation. "He wants you here, he's just a little unhappy with…with the problems we appear to be having."

"Then we need to try and put his needs before our own," Rachel said, a little more forcefully than she meant.

Jess frowned. It wasn't quite what she hoping for, but then again, she wasn't quite sure what she was expecting. "Yes, it would seem so."

Rachel stood. "That's settled then. Good."

"Wait. What happened yesterday, I mean, what went wrong?"

The confusion in those deep blue eyes was so evident. Rachel could easily believe Jess had no idea what she had done. "Do you really not know?"

Jess suddenly felt physically sick. *I've done something and forgotten again. This is a blinking nightmare.*

"No. Please Rachel, you have to tell me, I honestly don't. I never wanted to hurt you." She sighed. "Again."

Rachel was confused at the sincerity. "Jess, if you don't have any idea, maybe it's me that has the problem."

"Then why don't you just tell me? I'm sure we could sort it out." She was going to repeat that she loved her, but look where it got her the last time. She didn't intend making a fool of herself again.

"I don't know, Jess, I can't think at the moment. Let's just see how things go and think of Jack."

Jess swallowed and croaked, "Okay." She knew a brush-off when she heard one. She'd done it enough times herself. Maybe there was a glimmer of hope. Rachel was right, Uncle Jack came first. She potentially had all the time in the world to sort out her problems with Rachel. Her uncle's time was limited.

CHAPTER TWENTY-SIX

Jess watched as the flames began to ebb. The last week had seen some changes. Uncle Jack had experienced two bad days before they had managed to stabilize his pain relief. Since then he'd rallied and his mobility had improved. To Jess though, his condition appeared to deteriorate daily, although he and Tom would disagree with her as usual. The times she had spent with Rachel hadn't been many, but they had been reasonably relaxed and friendly. The only conversation they'd had though, had been over Uncle Jack, both were concerned regarding the trip down to London. Jess couldn't understand it, but she refused to argue with him if he wanted to attempt it. She picked up a couple of logs and tossed them onto the fire to bring it back to life.

She thought of her uncle and then of Rachel again. Despite their apparent ease the distance between them was growing. Jess ached for more. She attempted a smile to stop the sadness that was threatening to engulf her.

A gentle hand rested on her shoulder. "A penny for your thoughts?"

She looked up at her uncle. "There are too many of them. A penny is too cheap."

He wandered to the sofa and made himself comfortable. He then watched as his niece settled herself close to the hearth. "It's good to see you relaxing and thinking about something that brings a smile to that lovely face of yours."

She raised an eyebrow. "Do I normally look miserable then?" She realized her uncle was being serious when he shook his head.

"Oh Jess, I don't want to leave this world knowing that you are unhappy."

She took a deep breath, guilty for the pain she was causing. How had her life become so complicated? She shook her head, knowing she was just feeling sorry for herself. She smiled warmly. "I'm not really unhappy. I'm just confused."

"About Rachel?" She nodded reluctantly. "I want you to answer me honestly. Do you want Rachel in your life?"

She sighed. "Yes. Oh I don't know. Maybe what's happening is for the best."

"You do know that once Rachel leaves here that will be that, she won't be back."

Jess pounced. "Has she said something?"

"No, not exactly." He grinned. "I'm not manipulating you this time. I think I can guarantee it though, she won't be back next summer."

"I know she won't."

"Jess, it seems to me that Rachel is expecting you to take all the responsibility for what has gone wrong. She thinks that you should take the blame, and you're allowing her. She is either not the person I think she is, or she's expecting you to behave as Michelle Whitely did and can't see past that."

Jess sat up and looked at her uncle, surprised. Why hadn't she thought of that? She chuckled. "You're a wily old devil." Yes, she thought it natural Rachel would be sensitive, given her history, but to think she was Michelle all over again—it didn't please her, didn't please her at all. She frowned. "So what's my next move?"

He smiled happily. "You confront her. She has to know you are not fully to blame, and you have to find out why she walked away the last time."

"I've tried all that."

"No, Jess, I don't believe you have." Jess went to say something and her uncle stopped her. "You have to insist that she tell you exactly what has happened to make her act the way she has since your lunch."

"I can't do that. She may never speak to me again."

"And your point is? It may make her leave sooner rather than later, but you have absolutely nothing to lose. You are going to lose her anyway if you do nothing."

Jess sat back and closed her eyes. Moments passed before she said with determination, "I'll speak to her tomorrow."

CHAPTER TWENTY-SEVEN

"How did you find Rachel this morning?" Margaret attempted to brush the rain from her face. It was no use, she was soaked through.

Jess quickly finished wiping and packing away the tools, the rain hadn't stopped since the evening before. "Fine, why?" She lied.

"Oh, no reason, I just wondered." Jess looked at her questioningly. "Sorry, I shouldn't have asked. Can we get in the truck?"

Jess smiled. "Good idea."

They sat dripping in their seats with the rain hammering hard on the roof. "Is it worth trying to get these off?"

"No, one more stop I'm afraid. I bet you're glad you came along today."

Margaret chuckled. "When Rachel has work to do and is expecting phone calls, it's best to stay well out of the way, especially if that someone demands a lot of attention."

Jess grinned as she started up the engine. "Well, I'm glad I arranged to see her later then."

Margaret frowned. "Is everything all right?" She squeezed Jess's arm. "Don't answer that, I'm being nosy."

"It's okay. Is there something wrong? She did seem a little preoccupied. I put it down to the fact she was busy. That's why I'm seeing her later." She didn't add Rachel wasn't keen. But that didn't matter, Jess was determined.

"Oh, I think it's just me. She's just been a little subdued."

Jess thought there was more to it, but Margaret didn't add anything. She pulled up outside Broom Lodge. "Just logs to unload here, you stay out of the rain."

"A little late for that!"

Just as they closed up the log store, a ring from a Jess's mobile phone stopped them. She scrambled to retrieve it from her pocket. "Hi, Uncle Jack." Jess smiled at Margaret, relief evident on her face that it was her uncle on the other end. "We're just heading down for a hot drink and a dry out." She winked at Margaret. "Sorry, hang on, let me get in the truck, I can't hear you properly." It wasn't much better, but Jess concentrated on the call. "Yes, she's here." She turned to look at Margaret. "What!" The color instantly drained from her face.

Jess closed the phone and shoved it shakily into a pocket, then paused to calm herself. "Uncle Jack doesn't have any details at the moment, but Rachel has been involved in a car accident."

Margaret sucked in a horrified breath.

***

"Jess, be careful. Remember you have a passenger," Jack said through the open window of the truck.

"I will. Now please go inside, out of this rain."

Margaret leaned across Jess. "Yes, please Jack. We'll be all right, go inside."

Jack hadn't had any more information other than Rachel had been in a collision with another vehicle and had been run off the road.

Jess attempted to reassure Margaret and herself as she took off in the truck. "There are only ditches and fields on the way back from the village. The only drop is at Jock's Bridge and you can't go over it at any speed. I'm sure she's fine."

They sat in silence as Jess drove faster than either of them thought was probably best, though neither really cared. It felt like an eternity until Jess rounded a corner and muttered, "Please no."

Margaret could see the commotion at the end of the road. "That's the bridge isn't it?"

Bile burned the back of Jess's throat. She snatched a quick glance at Margaret while shifting up a gear. The look confirmed the question.

***

Rachel had been trapped, unhurt, in her Suzuki, between the embankment and a tree for nearly an hour. By the time she was freed and reached safety, she was wet, cold, relieved, but very angry. All she wanted to do was throttle the man who had been going far too fast to negotiate a bend in these conditions.

When Margaret and Jess pulled up, there was a police car, along with a fire engine, tractor and just ahead of that, an ambulance. The road was completely blocked.

Margaret instantly spotted Rachel. "Oh, thank God," she gasped and rushed over toward her, Jess following close behind. She grasped both Rachel's arms and quickly looked her up and down. "Are you all right?"

Rachel let out a breath, trying to calm her ragged nerves. "Yes, I'm okay."

"You gave us an awful scare." She stepped aside as Jess approached.

Rachel spotted the idiot in the other car and started to move in his direction. Another hand caught her arm. "Are you sure you're all right? Have you seen Tom or a medic?"

Rachel looked at the hand on her arm and then at Jess, trying not to look as angry as she felt. "Of course I'm sure. It was just a minor accident."

The hand kept a hold. "Minor in these conditions, it could have been...never mind, why aren't they checking you over, anyway?"

Rachel saw the man being helped into the back of a police car. Thanks to Jess she had missed the opportunity to give him a piece of her mind. "For heaven's sake, Jess, I'm fine. It's a country lane, not a damn motorway where idiots like him..." She looked in the direction of the police car. "Can reach speeds high enough to kill anyone."

Rachel felt the hand whip away, as if it had been scorched, just before Jess turned and walked briskly away. What she had said dawned on her. Horrified she cried, "Oh no, Jess, please. Please wait?"

A paramedic stepped in front of her, blocking her line of vision. "Ms. Cummings, could we please get you out of the rain?" She tried to get past him, only to see Jess break into a jog in the direction of her truck. "We really must check you over properly."

Suddenly exhausted and ashamed, she sighed and let herself be guided toward the waiting ambulance.

***

Julie jumped into the passenger seat and quietly said, "I thought you would have gone by now."

Through gritted teeth Jess said, "I brought Margaret here, I don't know if she needs a lift back."

Julie placed a hand on Jess's thigh. "I don't think she meant it, Jess."

"What the hell have I done to that woman? She hates me."

"She doesn't hate you, Jess. There's no way she hates you. Jess, I honestly don't think she meant it."

"Whatever I do is wrong. I've had enough. She doesn't have to put up with me anymore."

Julie sighed. "I'll go and ask Margaret if she is staying, or if she wants to go back."

Reaching the doors of the ambulance Julie tentatively knocked on the window. It opened and Margaret popped her head out. "Margaret, Jess asks if you require a lift back up to the lodges?"

Margaret hushed her voice. "They're worried about a head injury." She placed a hand on Julie's shoulder. "Thank Jess, very much. It's really very good of her. I'd better stay with Rachel."

CHAPTER TWENTY-EIGHT

Short of a few bruises and developing aches, Rachel was uninjured and discharged with advice for rest and gentle exercise. Margaret had hired a car, driven them home and ordered Rachel to bed until dinner.

Margaret smiled and indicated for Rachel to sit as she walked over to place two plates of food on the table. "How are you feeling? Better for the rest?"

"Yes. Thank you." Rachel was touched that Margaret showed nothing but concern when she surely had to feel disappointed in her. Why had it taken one of Jess's worst nightmares for her to wake up to what she was doing? Everyone had hinted at her to think, even Julie had this morning, when she took the package down to the post office.

She sighed looking at the one person who had helped her so much through her life. "Margaret, I've lied to you. I've lied to everyone, including myself, and worst of all, I've punished Jess for something that was my own fault." Rachel pushed her plate of food away and put her head in her hands. "I asked Jess to take me to bed, I practically begged her. She warned me it wasn't a good idea. That she couldn't because she would end up hurting me, but I still insisted." Rachel lifted her head. "I only thought of what I wanted and thought it was what she really wanted too. I didn't question her reluctance. I didn't ask why she thought she would hurt me."

Margaret reached across. "You said she didn't want a long-term relationship or commitment. That's why you didn't question it."

"No, Margaret. Even I should have known there was more to it than that. Her desire for me would have disappeared a long time ago if that was the true reason. She was afraid and I ignored that. Even when she explained it all to me, I ignored her. I have only thought of myself." Rachel faintly blushed at the admission and then swallowed hard. "The worst thing though, in this whole sorry mess, is that I don't believe Jess has ever once defended her actions. Not to me, not to Julie and not even to her uncle or Marie." Rachel's head dropped again in her hands as the tears started to flow in shame. She felt an arm slip around her shoulder and she accepted the hug she was pulled into.

It was a few minutes before Rachel leaned back and wiped away her tears. "You said to me right at the very beginning, not everyone is Michelle. I didn't listen to you then and I haven't listened to you since. When things went wrong, she was Michelle all over again. Jess is nothing like her. How could I ever have thought such a thing? What is the matter with me?"

"You've been hurt."

"Margaret, that's no excuse for how I've behaved." Watching her friend's face intently she asked, "Do I deserve Jess? Do I really deserve her?"

Margaret sighed. "I'm sorry, Rachel, you need to talk to Jess. Only she can tell you that."

***

Rachel pulled up the car in the only available space and ran through the front door of the house. People were everywhere.

"Rachel!" Jack beckoned her toward the lounge. "What on earth are you doing here? Margaret said you were supposed to rest."

Her heart raced faster as Marie and Julie just looked at her, saying nothing. "I came to see if Jess would speak with me."

"Well, I'm afraid she isn't here to ask at the moment."

"What's going on?"

"There's a small group of walkers who didn't show at the glen car park tonight. She is part of the search and rescue team. I'll certainly let her know you called in when she gets back."

Rachel frowned. "In this?" She waved her hand at the window that was being battered by wind and rain.

"It's nothing to worry about," Marie managed with a half smile. "Jess, Mark and the rest of the team are very experienced."

"They are very used to this kind of weather." Jack raised an eyebrow and grinned reassuringly. "Do we look worried?"

Julie glared at Rachel. "Well I'm worried. She wasn't in the best frame of mind."

Jack immediately shot her a look. "Jess wouldn't have gone out if she thought she was a risk to anyone else."

Julie nodded and sighed. "I know." She glanced at Rachel and muttered, "Sorry."

That didn't help Rachel. Julie was probably right, and all because of her stupidity.

Tom stepped forward. "You really should be resting. I'll take you back."

Rachel smiled. "Thank you, I can manage."

***

Just after midnight Rachel resigned herself to the fact that she wasn't going to hear from Jess tonight, if at all. Then the telephone rang.

"Rachel, it's Julie. I thought you ought to know. The team Jess is with has been out of radio contact for the last hour."

Rachel flopped down onto the sofa. "What...what do you mean?"

"It'll just be the weather conditions. Jack asked if I would let you know what was going on."

Rachel replied softly. "Thanks Julie, I appreciate it. What do we do, just wait?"

"Yes, I'm afraid so. Rachel...I'm sure Jess will be fine."

Margaret nudged her. "Remind them I'm a qualified orthopedic surgeon if they need help..."

"I heard that. Tell Margaret thanks. I'll keep in touch."

***

An hour later both Rachel and Margaret stared at the television screen wide-eyed in a desperate attempt to stay awake. They simultaneously jumped when the telephone rang again. "Rachel, Jess is fine but there are four injured people coming off the mountain with broken limbs. Tom is asking if Margaret wouldn't mind giving a hand?"

"Off course not, we'll be there immediately."

When Rachel and Margaret arrived people were scattering in all directions after what looked like a meeting on the porch of the house.

Tom immediately saw them and waved them over as he chatted to two people who stayed behind. "Margaret, Rachel, this is Ted and Audrey, our two paramedics. Apparently there is another team on the way."

After the introductions Tom explained the plan to Margaret. "Could you and Ted initially assess one of the injured walkers? His name is John. He seems to have been the leader in a group of four. He has no obvious head or internal injuries at present. He does have a shattered right leg, upper and lower, with possible hip and pelvis involvement. He also has a fractured right wrist and collarbone and a number of ribs." Margaret nodded. "If you could then deal with Mark, he is one of the rescue team. He has a fractured fibula, but is in a stable condition."

"The rescue team?"

"Yes. Afraid so."

"Okay, we can do that." She looked at Ted who confirmed.

"Good. Audrey and I will deal with the rest. Briefly, there's a walker with a fractured arm and collarbone. Another with a fractured wrist and ribs and then there are some minor injuries. Hopefully we won't get anymore, but they're navigating in thick fog now that the rain's eased off and it's still incredibly windy up there."

"All they need is for the snow to start falling. That'll have covered all the possible elements," Ted joked and received a raised eyebrow from Tom. "Sorry, Doc."

Tom continued. "If Mark's condition changes or you feel you're not able to attend to him quickly enough, give us a shout. The rescue team from the other side has joined ours, but they have allowed Jess to supervise the descent as she apparently had the situation under control after Mark's injury." He chuckled lightly. "Beware, she may be a little touchy, she doesn't like leading. Seriously though, she will be exhausted and will have a lot of information to relay to us. This is an unusual amount of injured; we need to pay strict attention. If any of us are struggling at any time we must immediately ask for help from each other. Okay?"

Margaret and the paramedics nodded in unison before they disappeared to make their preparations.

Tom turned to Rachel and smiled. "Don't worry, Jess will be fine, and you shouldn't really be out here after this morning."

Rachel didn't want to think of the danger Jess could be in. "Surely I could be of some help."

"I can't put this nicely, Rachel," Tom said. "We could do with your help, but when they get here, Jess is pivotal. She will be completely knackered and will need to concentrate on the status of injured and their priorities. You might be too much of a distraction."

Rachel nodded in resignation. "Maybe it would be best then if I..."

"Help me!" Julie butted in. "I'm going to struggle to direct the rescuers and walking wounded. They like to do their own thing."

Julie grabbed Rachel's hand. "Come on, I'll show you what's what." She explained the first stop would be the barn, and anyone who didn't need medical attention would be directed to the drying room. After which a nice cup of hot tea would be waiting in the dining room, organized by Marie and Jean. She emphasized the difficulty would be in getting them to move on. "Their adrenaline will still be pumping and they'll want to linger and that really isn't beneficial to the medics."

***

The next hour or so was bedlam. The team had been in constant contact on the way down from the mountainous terrain, relaying as much information as they could in regard to the injured. Once they reached their destination, Jess's priority was John, the male walker, and then Mark. She then relayed all the other injuries to Tom and Audrey. Jess was thankful it was all over and once things started to settle, she wandered over to see how her friend was bearing up. It could have turned out a lot worse than it had.

"Hi Jess. Doc, now that you've dealt with everyone else. I hope you are going to sort out our hero here?" Mark said as she approached.

Jess looked down at her leg, not comprehending at all what Mark was pointing at. Noticing the torn clothing matted with blood she felt instantly dizzy.

Margaret quickly sat her unceremoniously onto a nearby plastic chair and shoved her head between her legs. "Julie, could you come over here please?"

Jess started to raise her head. "It's all right, I think I feel okay."

Mark frowned at Margaret. "I think you better look at her arm as well. She may be the last, but she certainly isn't the least. You should have mentioned them, Jess."

***

Jess had persuaded Margaret to let her take a shower, soaking off the material adhering to her leg after the doctor had carefully hacked at all the layers of her clothing. It was wonderful to feel the warm water run over her body, rather than the cold sodden clothing fighting every move she made.

Out there tonight Jess decided life was far too short to be wasted. It needed grasping if you wanted the best out of it. If it didn't work out as you had planned, as least you could feel you'd tried. Rachel was all she had thought about.

They had fought to retrieve two people from a fragile shelf after the path they were walking along disappeared down the mountainside beneath them. Their partners had hopelessly looked on, not knowing whether to try and get help or stay. They stayed, knowing that they'd left in their car details of their route and how many were in their party. It was shortly after the rescuers arrived that the badly injured man's partner started to become angry, convinced his partner was going to die if they didn't hurry. He'd wished he had been more forceful in getting him to abandon the hike on such a dreadful day. Jess couldn't disagree with that. He then stupidly, when asked to stay put with his friend, approached a rescuer, again demanding to know why it was taking so long. The path slid away from under them, almost taking the two of them and Mark over the edge and to almost certain death.

Jess's anger for the idiot later dissolved after they'd secured everybody and the other team arrived. She'd watched him like a hawk, they all had, but when they brought his partner up, he burst into tears, blaming himself again. His injured partner did the same, for not discussing whether or not they should turn back when he became afraid conditions were too treacherous. He then couldn't stop apologizing for interfering and causing further injuries. He had never meant to hurt anyone. Jess had made sure someone stayed with him all the way down, reassuring him everything would be all right. It was good communication that had eventually seen them all to safety when conditions around them deteriorated.

Jess smiled thinking of Rachel again. She needed to talk to her.

***

Entering the bedroom to dress, she examined her wounds and decided both looked clean enough. Her arm harbored a deep scratch, which niggled a little. But her leg started to bleed again and she felt the need to support herself against the nearest wall. Grabbing several of the gauze swabs that Margaret had given her, she slapped them on her leg and bandaged them roughly in place. Her bed was looking very inviting as she forced herself out of the door. As she headed down she found the staircase difficult to negotiate, her leg throbbed on each step. The feeling was most unpleasant, so she gripped the handrail tightly.

Margaret smiled when she saw her coming and guided her over to one of the sofas. Jess was more than happy to relax into it and close her eyes. After a little muttering went on, Tom asked Margaret, "Are you sure you don't mind?"

"No, I have everything I need. You go home. You can examine my handiwork tomorrow."

"Goodnight Jess."

Jess didn't open her eyes. "Goodnight Tom. And thanks."

The room was silent and Jess sighed contentedly. Almost immediately she was aware of a presence and opened her eyes, meeting beautiful, brown ones. "Rachel."

"Hi. How does your leg feel? It looks pretty nasty."

"It's okay, but what's Margaret got in mind? Is it going to hurt?"

Rachel knelt down next to the sofa. "A little. Have you had stitches before?"

"Not the needle and thread type."

"You're quite the wimp, aren't you?"

Jess nodded with a sheepish grin. The eyes locked with hers were hypnotizing, but no matter how heavy Jess's became, she couldn't close them.

"I'm sorry, Jess. I'm so very sorry for what I said this morning."

The anguish in Rachel's eyes was so apparent Jess reached up and cupped her cheek. "You'd had a fright. It doesn't matter. I know you didn't really mean it."

Rachel sighed. "It does matter. I lashed out and upset you. Jess, I have a lot to apologize for." She placed her hand over Jess's. "We need to talk."

Margaret entered, pushing a trolley. "That leg of yours will need a rest and so will you." She looked at Jess. "Mind you, there's nothing to say it can't sit through a Halloween party tomorrow evening though, weather permitting."

Rachel and Jess looked at her and said in unison, "What?"

CHAPTER TWENTY-NINE

Jess lay in bed, feeling content. It was a far cry from the previous night when her exhausted mind had gone over the rescue and speculated over what Rachel might say.

Earlier in the evening, the occupants of Lomond Lodge and the house had ventured down to Bill's annual Halloween party after a very lazy day. Every year, weather permitting, there was a bonfire in the pub's back garden overlooking the river. Tables, benches and log burners were strategically placed around the extensive grounds. And the food was cooked outside on spits and barbeques. It was always a wonderful end to a busy season.

The day had been a beautiful one, after the deluge of rain the day before. The fire took a bit of persuading and a little extra fuel was needed to get it started, but eventually it roared into life and the night got underway. After eating with the others, Jess and Rachel wandered down to the river and only had to walk a short distance from the revelers to find a secluded bench with a wood burner glowing next to it. Jess chuckled to herself. *How convenient.*

Rachel had talked and Jess had listened. Rachel hadn't wanted to make Michelle an excuse for her behavior; she could have chosen to act differently. It became transparent to Jess as she continued to explain, that she lacked confidence when it came to sex, something Jess was already aware of, but she let her continue. Her trust in women, though, was nonexistent and Jess hadn't helped in that department at all. Despite that, Jess was pleased to hear Rachel say that the not-so-good parts of their relationship appeared so low due to the fact the highs were so good. She wasn't entirely sure she should be pleased, but she was.

All Rachel was saying she could relate to and understand where they had both gone wrong or misunderstood, except for one thing. What had happened the last time they had made love? Rachel had reiterated it was her mistrust, perceiving something to have happened that hadn't. She dismissed it as unimportant. Jess thought otherwise.

Rachel sighed. "Jess, would you allow a person to do something to you that you didn't want?"

"No, I wouldn't. Why?"

"I'm glad. You are a more honorable woman than I am."

To Jess, the look in Rachel's eyes showed she was someplace she didn't want to be. Rachel smiled wistfully. "I've spent most of my life thinking there was something wrong with me. I felt I lacked passion and a need for intimacy. I didn't enjoy lovemaking. I went through the motions and sometimes I could talk myself into enjoying it, just so that it wouldn't hurt."

"What do you mean, so that it wouldn't hurt?" Jess gripped her arm. "How could she not know? Some things you can't hide." Jess pulled Rachel gently to her. "I'm sorry. I wouldn't make a very good counselor would I?"

Rachel relaxed and settled into the safety of the arms around her. Jess knew exactly who she was talking about. "I learned how to make it easier, by fantasizing. It worked most of the time. You're right though, she did know it hurt at times." She let out a deep sigh. "But I didn't stop her either."

Tears welled in Jess's eyes. How could anyone treat such a wonderful woman so badly?

Rachel felt a tear trickle down her neck. "You'll probably find this hard to believe. I actually saw a therapist too, after my breakup with Michelle." She chuckled nervously. "Not that it appears to have done me any good, whatsoever." She looked up. "I come across the one person who gives me everything and I do my utmost to drive her away."

Jess smiled. "It'll take a lot more than your cold shoulder treatment to get rid of me now." She took Rachel's hand. "I think I've guessed what happened that afternoon." Pink colored Jess's face. "You might not find this easy to believe—I've never actually had anyone inside me."

Rachel gave a short gasp. "You had every right to stop me then." She grinned, more from relief than anything else. "But, you're right. I do find it difficult to believe that God's sexual gift to women has never let anyone slip these inside her." She wiggled both her eyebrows and two fingers for effect and it worked. Jess turned the color of beetroot. "Well stud, what's your excuse?"

"I usually find my pleasure in pleasuring others, that's more than enough for me. I like to be the one in control."

Rachel's smile grew serious. "I should have asked permission, as you did."

"I don't always ask permission. There isn't always a need. With you, what you wanted and didn't want was important to me."

"That should have been important to me too."

Jess chuckled. "You did ask. I said you could do anything. I was so turned on I was incapable of any coherent thought."

Rachel relaxed. "I can't believe I could get something so wrong." She looked into gleaming blue eyes that reassured her she didn't. "Jess, can we try and start from the beginning again?"

It wasn't quite what Jess wanted to hear, but she smiled, at least it wasn't a brush-off this time. As they stood to return to the others, Jess looked at Rachel and asked, even if it was to be their last, "Can I kiss you?"

"I thought you were never going to ask."

As she closed her eyes to sleep, she relived that kiss.

CHAPTER THIRTY

"Good morning. You two are up early." Jess beamed as she sat down at the breakfast table. "Something smells good."

The older residents of the house grinned at each other before they replied in chorus, "Good morning." Marie then excused herself to get washed and dressed.

Jack said, "I have some news regarding tomorrow." Jess looked at her uncle. Tomorrow was the day they would all be traveling down to London for Rachel's book signing event. "I know it's short notice, but I've decided it would be best not to go."

She was both relieved and disappointed. Pleased, as she thought the whole thing was a bad idea in the first place, yet upset that she wouldn't be spending the weekend with Rachel.

Jack smiled as if reading her mind. "The only reason I was going was so that you and Rachel would spend time together, and not make the break, an excuse to part company, forever."

She frowned. "Oh."

"Marie and I are more than capable of looking after the lodges and ourselves."

"Okay. If Rachel's still happy for me to go, then I will."

***

Jess accepted a glass of wine from the likable, stocky, dark-haired woman. Diane was everything Margaret had so lovingly described. "Thank you. You have a splendid home. The ceiling rose in my bedroom is amazing."

Diane smiled. "It is isn't it? I think it's the best one in the house. I hope you have everything you need. Margaret gave me strict instructions."

"It's perfect. When did you actually get back?"

Diane indicated for her to sit. "The day before yesterday. I'm glad I could escape in time for the book signing. It's going to be an important day for Rachel. The whole thing has just grown and grown."

Jess fidgeted a little apprehensively. "I'm not sure I've been to anything like tomorrow night's party." She laughed. "In fact, I know I haven't."

"You'll be fine, just be yourself. If I can get by in those things, you most definitely will. Margaret said you were a charming woman and that's all you need to be to survive one of these events." She winked. "And unfortunately, I have to agree and I don't like to do that too often."

Jess blushed. "You both must have agreed on Rachel. You all seem very close."

"Rachel is a lovely person, very easy to like. Yet, she has been let down by many people close to her. Even we've had our moments."

"Well, I'm glad she has the two of you, despite those." Jess smiled.

***

The rest of evening went well and Jess had been made to feel very comfortable. Despite the time the three women had known each other, they had included her wholeheartedly.

It wasn't a late night due to traveling and the early start for Rachel in the morning, but Jess couldn't help feeling disappointed with the outcome as the two of them made their way to their own bedrooms. She was more than happy, though, to take things slowly if that's what Rachel wanted. She just needed to practice a little patience. She smiled as she heard Rachel puttering around in their adjoining bathroom. After hanging the last of her items in the wardrobe, she removed her shoes and socks and waited on her bed for Rachel to finish.

"It's all yours." She quickly sat up in the hope Rachel would pop in, but she didn't. The other door was slightly ajar when she padded through to clean her teeth. She then called, "Good night."

"Jess?"

She stopped at the sound of her name and tentatively pushed the door so she could look into the room. "Yes?"

"Would you like to sleep in here, with me?"

Jess just stared, her eyes darkening. "Sleep would be the farthest thing from my mind."

Rachel suddenly felt a damp throb at her center. She took a step forward. "What's the nearest thing?"

"This." She took Rachel's lips with her own. It began slow and sensuous, but before long, lips and tongues danced feverishly.

Rachel could feel their bodies pulling and pressing harder together. Hands started to roam freely and Rachel became keenly aware she was being guided slowly toward the bed, her clothes being discarded piece by piece.

Out of breath and incredibly aroused, Jess was on the verge of climaxing. She pulled away and found herself straddling a naked Rachel. The eyes that looked up at her showed obvious need and surprise, even annoyance at the sudden withdrawal. Jess stared at the heaving breasts before her and muttered to herself, "How does she do this to me?"

Rachel blinked twice, trying to make sense of the quietly spoken words. "Do what?"

Jess was drowning in the woman beneath her. "What?"

Focusing on the blue dilated pools Rachel repeated. "What do I do to you?"

Jess looked puzzled and then smiled. "Did I say that out loud?"

Rachel pulled at her shirt, suddenly feeling a little self-conscious that the woman on top of her was still fully clothed. "Yes, unless I can read your mind."

"I'm reading yours." Jess lifted the garment over her head.

Rachel groaned at the sight of the toned form, as it lifted itself from the bed, removed all other remaining items hurriedly and returned to the straddling position.

Jess watched the brown eyes darken and glass over, fixing themselves on her breasts. Pulling her vision away, she admired every inch of the body glowing and subtly writhing between her legs. She lowered her head and grasped a nipple between her lips, pulling and teasing, before slowly kissing her way up to Rachel's ear. "What do you want?"

Rachel's breath hitched, the words tickling. She was so turned on she didn't know what she wanted. She just wanted this woman to touch her. "Oh Jess, don't torture me please."

"I don't want to torture you, just tell me what you want."

Rachel felt the body radiating heat above her slide down and press against her side. Next, she felt a hand brush over her breast and capture a nipple. Involuntarily, she rolled closer. "Please Jess, I need..."

"What do you need?"

Rachel lifted her hips as Jess lifted slightly over her and slipped a thigh between her legs. "Inside, I want to feel you inside."

Jess was delirious with desire. The moisture she felt as she pressed her thigh into Rachel's center was driving her senseless, now those words. She had to concentrate hard on providing exactly what Rachel needed. "Yes. Yes."

Rachel couldn't believe how desperate she felt. A hand was slowly and gently dancing down her body when she wanted it to hurry. It seemed like an eternity before it finally reached where she wanted it to be. She bucked, needing to come, yet the hand stroked teasingly, as if waiting for her to beg. As she rhythmically moved her hips, fingers slipped inside. She stiffened, waiting for the impending movement that would give her release, but it never came. Almost immediately, Jess's breathing increased and she moaned. Rachel squealed, "Stop."

It took Jess a moment, but she withdrew. "What, sorry, what have I done?" Panic in her voice.

Rachel sucked in a deep breath, pressing herself against the thigh still resting between hers. "Nothing, I need to touch you."

Jess's body was on fire, she wanted to take this woman in so many ways, and she just couldn't get enough of her. "No, I'll climax."

Rachel's eyes dilated. "I know. That's what I want. Both of us, at the same time, please. As soon as you make that one move inside me, I won't last."

Jess pulled Rachel over onto her side, caressing her back and kneading the soft buttocks, allowing her access to slide a hand between her thighs. Jess let out a deep guttural sigh at the touch. She was so close. Holding her breath in an attempt to control the inevitable, she whispered smiling, "I'm going in." Her fingers slid through Rachel's drenched and swollen folds.

"Oh yes."

As she moved rhythmically against Rachel and pushed deeper with her fingers, she heard, "Oh Jess, please, yes." Instantly a hand pressed and rubbed firmly over her clitoris as Rachel lifted her own hips off the bed in urgency. "Oh…"

Jess simultaneously felt her own center pulsate and moved in unison with the waves that gripped her fingers. "Oh yes…"

***

"Jess, are you with me?" Rachel circled a breast and a nipple slowly began to stand to attention.

"Just about," Jess said, looking up at the beautiful face hovering above her. "Not for long though, if you carry on like that." Rachel had driven her into a frenzy taking her so thoroughly with her mouth. She was convinced a heart attack or stroke was inevitable under this woman's attention, until her body exploded in release and her mind went completely blank.

Rachel stopped her movements. "You didn't answer my question."

Jess tried to think. It really wasn't any help. "What question?"

"The one I asked you." She glanced at the clock and smiled. "Four hours ago. What is it that I do to you?"

Jess grinned. "How much you make me want you. It's scary. You've turned me into a sex fiend that can't get enough of you."

"I don't know how I've managed that."

Jess continued, not thinking. "I know exactly how you did it. You made me fall in love with you. That's how." She'd said more than she intended to and cringed at her stupidity. She added lightly, "Well, you are rather wonderful, beautiful, gorgeous, in fact pure perfection. Even my uncle's in love with you. No one would stand a chance."

Rachel smiled. Jess had declared her love before, yet never mentioned it since. It was obvious to Rachel that Jess didn't want to pressure her into feeling the same way. How could she have ever doubted this woman?

"Jess I…"

Jess placed a finger on Rachel's lips. "Shush, don't say a word, there's no need." She watched the struggle on Rachel's face. She was so close to tears. "Come here, you have a long and important day tomorrow. Three hours sleep really isn't enough, but it's better than nothing."

Rachel snuggled in close and held on tight until sleep swept over her.

CHAPTER THIRTY-ONE

When Jess, Diane and Margaret arrived at Jasper's for lunch, Rachel and Scott were already seated and were deep in conversation. The signing was going well and Rachel had received a huge amount of interest over the illustrating. She was secretly pleased, but didn't want to encourage Scott any further with his gloating. She'd enjoyed the morning meeting fans, book lovers and colleagues. The only blight on the proceedings was Michelle, who had flirted, goaded and belittled her. Then, when Michelle amazingly declared they had made a mistake splitting up, Rachel had to laugh. She had done her utmost to ignore her, especially when it became apparent that there was more interest from book buyers over the illustrations than in the book itself.

It wasn't until they were just about to take a break for lunch that she realized how desperate Michelle actually was, when she suggested they tell the truth to the press. That they were in a long-term relationship and Rachel had left her. It would explain the dearth of her literary output over the last few years, which to Michelle's annoyance kept cropping up. She could just say she was heartbroken. That would get her a sympathy vote and hopefully boost her sales and status.

Rachel couldn't believe she'd ever contemplate such a scheme and wanted to say do I tell them why I left you? That was when she received her biggest surprise. She really didn't care anymore. Michelle being Michelle had no effect on her, the upset and anger she always felt in her presence just wasn't there. She smiled contentedly to herself. *You can never hurt me again.* She'd turned to Michelle and said, "All right. You can tell the world we were supposedly a couple, you with your many lovers and me foolishly hanging on to the one. It really doesn't matter to me." Scott and Michelle's agent had been in earshot. Scott smiled. Michelle and her agent glared at her. *Neither, can you use me.*

***

Rachel quietly entered her bedroom planning a bath before the party, unless Jess was sleeping. When she'd arrived back her friends had confessed they thought they'd worn Jess out shopping. Margaret suspected Jess's leg was bothering her and she just wanted a little time to herself before the evening got underway. If Jess was resting, she would rest for a short while too.

She was disappointed not to see Jess in her bed. Noticing the adjoining doors to the bathroom were open, she tiptoed through and peered into the other bedroom. Jess was lying on her side, propped up on her elbow and grinning. "I'm awake."

Rachel was struck by how magnificent she looked, the simple pair of jogging shorts and a T-shirt emphasizing her long, lean body.

Jess was lost in Rachel's gaze, enjoying the fact she was openly admiring what she saw. Rachel approached her and cupped Jess's cheek before tilting her head and pouting her lips slightly. "Ah, you poor thing, did they wear you out?" Rachel squealed as Jess grabbed her wrist.

"I'll show you who's tired." She winced and then she looked Rachel up and down. "Um, I'd better let you go. Your dress?"

"I'm not worried about the dress. I'm more worried about your leg. It's bothering you, isn't it?"

"A little, but it's fine. I'll have a bath before we go out. That should help."

Rachel wasn't convinced. She smiled wickedly. "If I take off my dress, will you take off your bandage?"

Jess laughed and unraveled the bandage. Her leg was a little red and swollen. "Tom gave me antibiotics as a precaution. I'll let Margaret take a look and let her decide if I should start taking them."

"Now let me take a look at your arm." Rachel stroked gently down the side of the six-inch long graze. "That looks okay." She slowly traced a finger upward and around slightly parted lips, her eyes following every movement. She said teasingly, "All right?"

Jess swallowed hard, waiting for whatever Rachel had in mind. Her body started to crave a lustful dance and this was not the time to take the initiative. Rachel was on a high and feeling incredibly bold. She closed her eyes and slid further up onto the bed, looking forward to the outcome.

Immediately she was straddled. She tugged at Rachel's silk slip. "What do you have under here?" She knew exactly what was under there. She could see the outline of the lace bra and her fingers had glanced over the edges of lace panties and a suspender belt as she rested her hands on Rachel's hips. Usually, those did nothing for her, but Rachel wearing them was a totally different concept. The slip was then lifted and removed. "Oh God," was all she could manage.

Rachel smiled. She could feel the heat building and see the chest rapidly rise and fall in the stunning creature trapped between her thighs. She resumed her tracing, outlining the collar of Jess's T-shirt and moving down to between her breasts. Pinching at the material and letting it drop, she repeated Jess's words. "What do you have under here?" She too knew the answer, it was plain to see, absolutely nothing. Her gaze drifted upward to meet glassy, hooded eyes and recognized that look of wanting and desire.

Jess croaked, "Kiss me." And as Rachel lowered her head she was pulled into a passionate tussle of lips and tongues.

Jess arched her back and moaned as Rachel pulled away and lowered her head, slowly making a trail of kisses down an extended neck, shoulders and finally brushing the hard, pink nipples that were in danger of pushing through the material.

She continued to tease her way lower until she reached the area that most needed her attention, Jess writhing beneath her. She pulled at the waistband of Jess's shorts and slid them down as she lifted her hips off the bed. Once they were discarded she slowly kissed her way back up to the top of her inner thigh and stroked with her tongue. She heard a high-pitched groan as Jess bucked. She then twirled her fingers around the swollen folds. Jess was so wet, open, and in great need.

Rachel's arousal reached fever pitch. Again she was amazed at the trust Jess had in her as she fleetingly contemplated sliding her fingers in. She had wanted to more than once last night. It would be easy to convince herself that Jess was begging her to do it with every thrust of her pelvis. She wanted to hear a voiced invitation, not one she thought was being asked for in the heat of passion. It had to be right.

The hunger and need continued to course through Rachel as she found herself on the verge of her own orgasm. In danger of coming first, she clasped her mouth to Jess, sucking and flicking until Jess cried out her name. Her own body pulsated as pressure was released.

Jess opened her eyes to find Rachel cradled in her shoulder. The giddiness, the sound of rushing blood through her ears, and the sweat escaping from every pore, slowly subsided.

Rachel looked up at her, a self-satisfied grin on her face. Jess narrowed her eyes. "Smugness doesn't become you. Rachel, I..." She didn't get very far before she was pushed down and a smiling face once again looked up at her.

"I know you enjoyed it and I have every right to be smug." The fleeting doubt Rachel felt had gone. Jess went to say something but a barring finger was placed on her lips. "The last couple of days have been bliss. Thank you." Rachel caressed her cheek. "I hope it will continue. A good woman, good sex, what more could I ask for? Oh yes, to be a contributing artist at the National Gallery. How's that for a life?"

Jess blinked twice. "What did you say?" Rachel beamed as Jess rose onto her side. "The National Gallery, you're exhibiting at the National?"

Rachel squealed and slapped Jess on the hip. "Yes!"

Pulling her into a tight hug, Jess responded excitedly, "That's wonderful, congratulations!"

"I knew you'd be pleased for me."

Jess pulled away, her eyes glistening brightly, amazed that this woman could give off the air of confidence, yet at times appear so vulnerable and insecure. "Of course I'm pleased for you. What an accolade. And one you deserve, I might add."

CHAPTER THIRTY-TWO

Jess threw another couple of logs onto the fire before refilling her wineglass and then slumped lazily back into the overstuffed chair. She listened to Uncle Jack's groans and protestations as the nurse bathed and readied him for bed. Marie didn't like this part of the day, feeling the hopelessness of the situation. After the arrival of Nurse Pat, as Marie called her, she had taken to spending the night with Bill. He would collect her after dinner and return her early the next morning.

The few weeks since her visit to London had seen a rapid decline in his health and they all knew it was only a matter of days before, as Jack would put it, he'd be meeting up with the family and his Mary. Don and Jean had emigrated as planned, Jack had insisted they go and not wait around for the inevitable.

Business at the lodges had continued as it had last winter and summer, and according to the bookings, there would be no quiet period ahead.

Jess, with her uncle's help, had tried to plan for the future. She had looked into hiring a manager and contractors to carry out maintenance. She'd also spoken tentatively to Mark. His daughter, Emma, had arrived home shortly after graduating in business studies with a baby in tow and no man on the horizon. He hadn't been pleased, but his granddaughter was beginning to win him over and it didn't look as if Emma was in any hurry to move on.

Rachel had been busy since the signing. Although every spare few days she had, she had been here. Most of her time was spent either in London or New York. Rachel was happy, if not a bit travel weary, and Jess couldn't deny her that. She couldn't expect Rachel to give that up just for her. So Jess had decided she would follow Rachel, if she would allow it. She could live like that if she made an effort. She took a gulp of wine. But she loved the lodges...*I love Rachel more.* Her thoughts, as they drifted to the beauty that'd changed her life completely, were interrupted. "Jess, Jack's settled. If you don't mind, I'm going to have a bath and then get an early night?"

Jess smiled. "Thanks, Pat. I'll see you in the morning."

***

Jess tapped on the door. "Uncle Jack?"

His eyes fluttered open. "Jess, come in. Sit down and keep that woman away from me."

They both chuckled. Pat had been such godsend since her arrival over two weeks ago.

"You know what the best thing about today was, Jess?"

"No. What?"

"I'm now convinced I'm going to leave you happy."

He patted her hand. "And one more thing, don't worry about this place. Don't feel you have some obligation to me to keep it going. I mean it Jess, This place was Mary's dream, then mine. I know you love it, but it is only a place. I would have gone wherever Mary wanted to go, done whatever she wanted to do. I want you to know, you have that freedom too." He grinned. "I don't want you fearing that I'll come back and haunt you if you sell."

She smiled warmly. "We'll see, but thanks."

They were quiet for a few moments, both listening to the owls calling to each other in the darkness. Jack queried, "Rachel is coming back tonight isn't she?"

"Yes, she is. Even though I asked her if she would stay in a hotel overnight and drive up in the morning. She'll be tired from the flight."

"She'll be fine. She sleeps well on planes." Squeezing her hand, he asked, "Will you stay with me tonight, Jess?"

She looked at her uncle knowing why he had asked and softly replied, "Yes."

***

Jess had been awake for four hours, watching her uncle like a hawk, remembering his words. He wasn't afraid to die, though he wasn't keen to do it alone. She desperately tried to get herself to relax again so he wouldn't pick up on her anxiety. She was only tired, and he deserved to go peacefully, if that's what this was all about. She sighed. *I don't want you to go.*

A car door slammed and Jess could feel her tension instantly ease. She whispered, "It's Rachel, Uncle Jack. She's back."

Jess heard the bare feet patter on the stairs and then along the landing. Still watching her uncle's breathing she called out quietly.

Rachel's head bobbed around the door and concern was instantly recognizable on her face. "Jess, what's going on?" She walked over and rested a hand on her shoulder.

Jess reached up and held it, smiling up at her. "Uncle Jack's sleeping. He didn't want to be alone. It's good to see you."

Rachel glanced at Jack and then back at Jess before bending down for a kiss.

Jess moved her hand to the back of Rachel's head and pressed harder. She tasted so good and Jess relaxed completely. She wanted more, a giddy feeling starting to overwhelm her. Rachel dropped to her knees and caressed Jess's cheek. "I'm not sure this is quite the right place."

Jess looked down at her hand still holding onto her uncle's and then to his face. "He wouldn't…"

A slight smile adorned his features. His breathing had ceased.

CHAPTER THIRTY-THREE

The funeral was not too somber. In fact, Jess had quite enjoyed it. Everyone there seemed to have a story to tell about Jack and it was lovely hearing them all. Jack had organized his finances and wishes perfectly, so solicitors were not slow in organizing and carrying them out despite the Christmas and New Year holidays. Jess was tired and needed a rest. Today it felt like it had all caught up with her and she was exhausted. She also felt the need to talk to Rachel, to see what her plans were before she disappeared again.

Jess sighed and then relaxed as she gazed up at the snow-covered peaks, basking in sunshine. This was a complete contrast to yesterday, when they just disappeared into the gray and murky sky. She jumped at the sound of the reception bell and called, "It's okay, Marie, I'll get it."

As Jess approached the area the bell sounded again, the user obviously losing patience. She recognized the mousey-featured man as a previous patron. She welcomed him back, booked him in and relayed all the necessary information for an enjoyable and safe holiday. The whole time the man glared at her and continued to show his impatience with a continuous, "Yes, I know."

Jess remained poised. Maybe he'd had a bad journey, his wife and three children testing him on the long drive. "I think that's everything, sir. Would you like me to show you to your lodge?"

"No, that's fine, I know where it is and if I have any problems with anything I'll get back to you. In fact, my wife is worried this place won't be the same."

Jess frowned. "Why? Maybe I can help?"

"She heard the old man that owned the place died. Is that right?"

Anger, hurt, disappointment, wanting and loss, all slammed into Jess as if she had suddenly hit a brick wall. Her head instantly throbbed with the ball of rage that instantly consumed her. *Old man. Old man. Died. And they're worried about their bloody holiday.*

"I hope the new owners haven't changed anything, he ran the place so well."

New owners, there aren't any new owners, you idiot.

"It's often the case when this sort of thing happens and the holiday you hoped for never materializes. I hope that won't be the case here."

How can things change so quickly, how can he be dismissed so quickly.

Rachel couldn't believe what she had heard or how rude and thoughtless a person could be. Marie had asked her to come through and see if Jess would be showing them to their lodge before the three of them had lunch. The man was looking at Jess for reassurance.

"I can assure you, your holiday won't be affected, sir."

Rachel noted Jess's tone and watched her follow him to the door and tightly grip its edge. When the man disappeared Jess stood unmoving. Something wasn't right. "Jess." No response. "Jess."

Jess turned slowly around. She'd heard her name, yet it seemed so distant. Everything started to spin uncontrollably. She had to escape before she was sucked into the impending vortex.

Rachel instantly recognized the vacant, unseeing look. Those dark, frightened eyes were the same as she had seen that *night*.

Rachel moved as quickly as she could, spying Jess as she disappeared behind the barn. Panting, she rounded the building. *Great, up the hill*. As she started up, she couldn't believe her luck. Jess had slipped in mud and in her panic was unable to get a clean footing.

"Jess, please. Please stop?"

Jess didn't move. She could hear a voice and it sounded familiar. Why would that be in the storm that was raging about her? As her head pounded, her hand and knee throbbed in unison. She concentrated on the voice, it sounded calm. Firm, soft hands cupped her face. "It's Rachel, my darling, it's all right, everything's all right."

Looking around her, puzzled, Jess asked, "What's going on?"

Rachel spoke quietly. "That idiot of a man upset you."

His words flooded Jess's senses and the emotions she'd held inside erupted like a volcano. She shrieked, "It's all so bloody final, like he never existed."

"No Jess, that's not true, he will always be here." Rachel pressed a hand to Jess's heart before pulling her into a tight hug. Her own tears flowed, but nothing in comparison to the sobs escaping the woman she was holding.

As Jess's tears slowly abated, she met Rachel's eyes. "I promised myself I would never run from you again." Her head still pounding, she dropped her eyes in shame.

Rachel hugged her closely again and replied, "You didn't run from me, Jess. You ran from the words of a fool and your grief. Not me."

***

Rachel sighed as she watched Jess open the wine, she still looked out of sorts. She had slept all afternoon and then insisted on cooking them a meal, saying she would sleep better tonight.

Jess handed her a glass. "Why the sigh?"

"Oh…Scott's been on the phone. He wants me back in London."

"When and for how long?" Jess hoped she sounded casual.

"Tomorrow, I'm afraid, but back by the weekend." Rachel saw the disappointment in Jess's face. She was disappointed too, but there was nothing she could do. Not this time, anyway.

Jess sat down and looked at Rachel, it was obvious she regretted having to go so soon, but what choice did she have? It was her work. She had a choice though. She smiled. "Good, I'll take the weekend off." In the meantime, she had some planning to do.

CHAPTER THIRTY-FOUR

As Jess looked out the landing window she caught sight of Rachel rounding the corner of the house. She ran down the stairs. She couldn't help it. Her grin was wide when she opened the door. "Hi." It came out as a squeal.

Rachel grinned back. "Hi, to you too. And why did I get a cryptic message from Marie when I arrived, asking me to be here at seven?"

"Dinner." Jess swallowed and stepped aside.

Rachel had known the look she would be greeted with, and there it was, heated and scanning her hungrily from top to toe. She took a step closer and smiled seductively, hoping there was no stoic will left in the woman she had her eyes on. She needed

Jess's touch, anything, in fact, to release the increasing and painful pressure that was building so rapidly within her. She glanced at the sofa along the back wall of the kitchen and then back to Jess. "Aren't you pleased to see me?" She knew she was being cruel. It was obvious Jess had a plan for the evening and this wasn't it. Not yet, at least.

Jess closed her eyes in a failed attempt to relax. Managing a smile, she closed the gap between them. "Of course I'm pleased to see you. Welcome back." Her lips softly took Rachel's, and her hand slipped to her waist, trembling. She meant for it to be short and sweet, but when she tried to pull away, Rachel wouldn't let her. The kiss deepened as their lips pressed together more urgently. They both started to fight for possession as bodies moved in desperation and hands became frantic and greedy in their need to feel and roam.

Rachel eventually pulled away, breathless and wanting more. She croaked, "Please, Jess I need you to do something. And now." She then guided her toward the sofa, pulling at her clothes.

Jess groaned whilst she fumbled at buttons that were getting in the way of where she wanted to be. Eventually she slipped a hand in the front of Rachel's dress and under her camisole, cupping a breast that filled her hand. She felt dizzy as her palm rubbed over a large hardened nipple.

While lips continued to urge, caress and taste, Jess slipped her other hand between Rachel's thighs. She mumbled between breaths and kisses. "Oh Rachel, you're so wet."

Rachel immediately responded to the touch and heated words, bucking to push the hand hard against her aching groin. She felt her panties being pushed to one side as Jess continued to stroke and tease. She raised her hips again, wrapping a leg around Jess's back and gripping onto her shoulders to pull her closer. She was rewarded with what she so desperately wanted. Fingers slipped inside her. She threw her head back, tightly gripping the shirt clenched in her fists. "Oh yes, yes, don't stop." Each movement was ecstasy before her body stiffened and then pulsated with every wave of pleasure that washed over it.

She lay there for only a moment before another surge of arousal gripped her. Jess rhythmically moved herself against her thigh in unison with her fingers that were still softly enveloped in her moist, swollen tissue. She bent her leg as Jess's thighs grew tighter about hers and started pushing it harder against Jess. Her hands curled through the red mass of hair resting on her chest and she could hear breathing becoming more and more labored. Rachel relished the feeling of desperation in them both, her climax impending, yet again. Pulling Jess's head up, her mouth settled close to an ear and in an urgent whisper she said, "Come with me, Jess."

That's was all the encouragement Jess needed to send her over the edge, one last push together, and they both cried out at the same time. They lay there quietly for a few minutes both catching their breath and relishing the feel of one another.

Jess was the first to break the silence. "Well, so much for my slow seduction over a romantic dinner."

***

Rachel flopped onto the armchair and sighed contentedly. "That was a beautiful meal." She watched Jess poke aimlessly at the fire.

"Rachel, I've been thinking…"

"Yes?" She waited, but Jess didn't continue. They had chatted easily throughout dinner. It was only when they'd decided to tidy up and adjourn that Jess appeared distant and thoughtful. "About anything in particular?"

Jess put the poker down and turned toward Rachel. "I don't know how else to say this, so I'm just going to say it." As Jess took a deep breath, Rachel felt a little alarmed. "I love you and I hate when I'm not with. I miss you when you're not here. I want you to share my life and I want to share yours. And if that means living in New York, I will do it. I will go anywhere, if it guarantees being with you."

Rachel was overwhelmed by the rushed words. "You would?"

"Yes," Jess said, relieved.

It was exactly what Rachel wanted to hear, even though it obviously hadn't come out quite as Jess had rehearsed. She smiled wickedly to herself. She couldn't help it and wanted to see if she had really thought it through. "Jess, your home is here, not in New York, or anywhere else for that matter."

"I can't pretend I know what it would be like to live over there. I'm certain I could adjust, if it meant spending more time with you." Jess couldn't help feeling a little anxious. "I can manage not to work, money isn't a huge problem. I wouldn't want you to think I would be bored, though. I have looked into a number of opportunities, and I'm aware they have city rangers. There are also a number of companies who provide walking breaks and they say they are always looking for experienced guides. It would mean being away, but only for a few days at a time. I was hoping though, you'd still wish to come here for most of the summer?" She looked for some reassurance.

Rachel fought back the sudden swell of emotion. Jess had thought about this. *Why did I doubt it?* She nodded and continued to listen.

"I've also looked into a number of alternatives for running this place, either employing more staff, or as Emma has said, if need be, she would oversee contract staff. The firm I've looked at comes highly recommended. It shouldn't be too much of an issue." She smiled, beginning to relax. "Marie doesn't mind doing spot checks either, especially on the weekend changeover of guests. She said she may struggle to let go of this place once she and Bill are married, despite expanding into bed-and-breakfast at the pub. It suits me, I'll soon know if our standards are dropping. I think Marie will soon settle though and that pleases me more."

Rachel swallowed hard. "You've looked into everything?"

From her tone, Jess thought she was either surprised, or having difficulty composing herself. "What are you thinking?" The brown eyes she searched suddenly filled with tears.

"You belong here, not in a big city." Rachel shook her head, tears flowing freely. "Come here." She opened her arms and waited for Jess to fall into them. "I do love you, so very much. I'm lucky to have had you come into my life, Jess Brewster."

Jess beamed, brushing away the tears. "Nah, I'm the lucky one. I wasn't even looking to share my life and now that you're here, I wouldn't want it any other way."

Rachel smiled, the tears subsiding. "Neither of us is going anywhere. I'm moving in with you, whether you like it or not. You can't work just anywhere, I can. You belong here and that's final."

Jess raised an eyebrow in mock disapproval. "So that's it then, I don't get a say?"

Rachel shook her head. "I've made arrangements with Scott to cut my schedule considerably, and I'm renting out my flat in New York. I will expect you to accompany me on some engagements though. So that had all better be to your satisfaction, madam?"

"You've done all that?" Rachel nodded. "Well, I don't know what to say."

"Just say you agree."

Jess searched Rachel's eyes for a moment and then moved to her lips. Rachel instinctively licked them before they were captured in a long, sensual kiss. "I agree," she whispered in Rachel's ear. "Now, please, will you make love to me?"

Goose bumps traveled down Rachel's body. She took Jess's hand. "With pleasure."

***

It wasn't long before they were naked and passionately embraced on the bed, both of them panting and bodies glistening with sweat. Fingers waded through Rachel's hair after another bruising kiss. "Oh Rachel, please..."

Rachel teased her way down the undulating body, capturing a nipple between her lips and circling a taut and flat abdomen with her hand.

Jess fingered Rachel's hair again and pressed her hard to her breast. She was so turned on and so very close. "Rachel, please hurry, or it will be too late."

The intensity of movements below her and the hands on her head, never mind the strangled words, sobered Rachel a little. It would be all over before she had her chance. "Hold back a little longer, darling." She slowed her explorations and then purred, "I want this to be perfect."

Rachel kissed the base of her pubis, careful not to touch

the engorged clitoris. She looked up and watched as she slowly stroked the swollen wet folds before gently sliding a finger in.

They both moaned. "Oh yes." She slid the finger out and then in deeper again. Jess stiffened. Rachel asked breathlessly, "Are you all right?" She heard a deep, "Yes," as she felt Jess arch again, attempting to push her further inside. As the rhythmic urgency continued, Rachel took the opportunity to insert another finger. She sighed at the feeling and heard Jess cry, "Oh yes." She looked up to see a face full of need and wanting at her touch. Desire rushed through Rachel as the rocking continued, her climax pulsating with every move.

Jess didn't want this feeling to end, the pleasure Rachel was giving her was intoxicating and she wanted it to go on. But her body couldn't hold out any longer, her head would either explode or a blood vessel would rupture. She thrust forward one last time before her body stiffened and she gasped, "Rachel, yes, yes. Oh yes, Rachel..." She slumped back onto the bed, blood rushing through her ears, lights twinkling in her eyes and her lungs burning as she tried to get a breath.

Rachel just waited, watching in awe, relishing each time she felt a contraction grip her fingers. Tears welled at the sheer joy and pleasure this woman had shown her.

Jess attempted to focus on Rachel. "You've killed me haven't you? I've died and gone to heaven." Jess heard a sniff then felt a tender kiss on her cheek.

"Relax, everything's perfect, you must have got used to my tears of joy. I'm getting used to your unresponsiveness when I've made love to you."

Jess smiled. "Sorry and thank you."

Rachel nestled into her. "Anytime."

Jess felt herself drifting. "Rachel?"

A sleepy voice responded. "Yes."

"You've ruined me, you know. I love you so much that I can't imagine being without you. Who would have thought it?" She then grinned and answered her own question, "Everyone but me it would seem."

Rachel snuggled closer. "You don't have to imagine life without me. You're stuck with me, now and forever."